A Long Reign
The Society Travelers Series, v.1

Victoria L. Szulc

Copyright © 2017, 2022 Victoria L. Schultz/Hen Publishing, a Hen Companies Brand

All rights reserved. Although there are references to actual historic events, places, and people, all of the characters, places, and dialogue in this book and its related stories, are fictitious, and any resemblance to any person living, dead, or undead is coincidental.

A gentle word to my readers/trigger warning: *although my pieces are works of fiction, my books and stories contain scenes and depictions that may upset certain audiences.*

Cover Photography/Art Direction: Victoria L. Szulc, on location at the Campbell House Museum, St. Louis, MO

Cover Design: Michele Berhorst

Model: Mary L. Poll

ISBN-13: 978-1-958760-05-5

ACKNOWLEDGMENTS

Special thanks to my family and friends. Your support helps me fulfill my dreams.

TO THOSE WHO HOLD OUT FOR HOPE.

For their dreams and faith keep the world alive.

PROLOGUE-A THIEF IN THE NIGHT

New Year's Eve – 1899

I had heard many stories about how the Traveler was stolen from the Society. But what I'm relaying to you here is certainly the most credible tale.

On New Year's Eve of 1899, a delivery man arrived at an ostentatious compound of distinctly manors, an impressive hall, and grounds of grandeur. This man's arrival was expected, for he was considered a Fixture of the organization that owned the whole territory. This organization, the Society, one that I am now a part of, had been developed long ago to act for "the greater good".

The driver passed through the ornate gates in an ordinary delivery carriage. Inside the transport was an incredible cake, created for a once in a lifetime evening. A guardian of the dessert, in the form of a baker, also a Fixture, sat next to the impressive sweet. A new century was coming, and the compound's inhabitants were ready to celebrate.

But the cake wasn't of the most importance to the driver or the baker. What they were going to replace the cake with that evening, would temporarily change the world for fifty years.

The driver, Mr. Stuart, was of Germanic heritage. He had a bushy dark beard and mustache that was behind the times in fashion. I would later find out that he was truly only known by his last name, Ebersol. The baker's name was Dr. Carthage. Ever since word of a possible time travel device reached an opposing organization to the Society, the Mass, the two men had been recruited to steal it for the not so greater good.

Revelers lined the streets as they entered the secretive grounds that were a satellite location for the most powerful spy organization in the world. The holiday was a perfect distraction for their plan. The massive five-tier cake was delivered and put in place at 10 p.m. Its size and weight had been carefully calculated to match that of what would soon go into the truck.

Members of the Society delved into the cake's luscious layers of rich delight, as the driver and baker were invited to join in the celebration and roam the grounds in return for their savory efforts. There were carriage and horse rides all over the grounds, so their covert trip to find Wilson Manor and its basement lab was hidden in plain sight.

By the time most of the St. Louis Society Members tucked into bed at the dawn of a new century, Ebersol and Dr. Carthage had the Traveler boxed and prepared to ship to England.

Their ruse changed my life forever. Twice.

CONTENTS

	Acknowledgements	iv
	Prologue-A Thief in the Night	v
1	On the Surface	9
2	In the Thick of Things	13
3	Other Things of Note	23
4	Discovered	26
5	How to Speak English	42
6	Below the Surface	58
7	A Word About the Captain	71
8	Passages	79
9	Bitter Harvest	92
10	The Maker	101
11	Learning Curve	105
12	Derailed	112
13	Ebersol	120
14	Roles	132
15	Infiltration	140
16	Back Forward	149
17	The Past Never Happened	163

1 ON THE SURFACE

London, 1919

Today I awoke with the stereotypical butterflies in my gut. I have been training for this day since I was fourteen.

I bounced out of bed with nervous anticipation. My skin warmed with the glare of the rising sun through the dirty window. I briefly peeked out at the sordid neighborhood below. The acrid smell of trash in the streets assaulted my nostrils when I lifted the sash. Filthy children skipped along the garbage and sludge while their mothers screeched at them to stop playing and hurry off to school before the Redcoats saw them, or heaven forbid, kidnap the poor kids.

I had hoped that an overnight rain would have cleared the air. Instead, the humidity only intensified the muck and squalor of the slum in which I'd been hiding.

This beat up flat was just temporary accommodations. I had fully adjusted to a wealthier lifestyle but hadn't forgotten what it'd been like to do without. So, I still managed to get a decent sleep in a room with only pieces of tattered furniture and paint peeling from the walls.

I threw on my under dress and wound a slim gadget belt around my body. I gazed in the cracked mirror on a plain dresser. I was dangerously fit, yet plump in the right places.

I leaned in and applied my make up with great care. Not too gaudy, not too thin. I needed to look good, but not ostentatious. No one should outshine the Queen, especially on her one hundredth birthday. I topped off my look with a pompadour and one very special hair comb accessory.

My boots came next. Super thick soles, with pricey copper tips hidden inside the toes of the leather. They were created especially for me. I tugged on the laces with a grimace. It had taken two agonizing weeks to break them in without anyone knowing.

As I opened the creaky closet door, it whined as if it didn't want to give up the incredible pale pink gown it stored. The lace around the high collar tickled my jawline.

A last look around the spare room reminded me of exactly what I needed to do. The have nots would soon be a thing of the past. Order eventually restored, perhaps. So far from the days when I was a slave in the former Americas.

They say the Queen hadn't been the same since Albert had died. Certainly no one is spared from the painful death of a loved one. At first, she'd become more reclusive. Always in black, only appearing for the most important of events. Then foul tempered and far more demanding.

However, the tragedy did end up uniting the world. The sun would never set on the British Empire. The retaking of America in 1864 was a brilliant stroke of military genius. The Spanish and French were made generous offers for their help. In return, America's Civil War ended by Presidents Lincoln and Davis surrendering all to the great Monarchy of Mother England.

Those days were particularly hard ones for my parents, who had married in their early teens at the start of the War Between the States. The South was already bloodied and broken. The North had lost faith in its president. The United States had been like an open wound, bleeding excessively and ripe for infection. The country collapsed soon after.

Davis was hanged for treason even though he'd just tried to persuade the Queen to join the South in its efforts to secede from the Union. Lincoln caved to the pressure to save America of her young dignity and agreed to rule over Western England as Lord Lincoln. He too changed. Eventually he became lazy and portly. His generals and colonels controlled the territories. The world had become one big Kingdom.

Redcoat soldiers roamed the streets, especially at curfew. Fields were stripped of their last harvest and sent off to feed the new military. Food was strictly rationed for over ten years. The lack of nourishment delayed my mother's ability to get pregnant until her mid-thirties and even then, it was a complete surprise.

As a child, I never forgot the rumble of my insides as I could only have one meal of soup and bread a day. Milk was reserved for special occasions. I learned to farm, clean, cook, sew, and trade, all before the tender age of ten.

Fortunately, I was seen as a miracle and treated as such. Neighbors went to incredible lengths to make sure I was properly educated even if I couldn't eat well. Books were smuggled in under old rags. Their pages were like gold to me. My body was thin, but my mind was sated.

Despite my lean figure, I had one gift that drew the attention of a particularly astute Redcoat Captain. I was beautiful. I had light brown hair with shimmers of red gold, deep blue eyes, and an infectious smile with dimples.

Captain Braden Davis had noticed me working in the cornfields of Missouri after he'd been assigned to St. Louis. It was a position he had hoped to secure for years, for the area was rife with rebellion. The Captain was part of an uprising that he had desperately developed in other cities and even across the ocean in the World Capital of London. After successfully infiltrating the military, he discovered what all of us had suspected. That something had long been amiss with the Queen. Prince Albert's demise was not of natural causes. The poison that killed him was meant for the Queen. And we, being the Underground of the former United States of America, were prepared to find out exactly what had gone horribly wrong with our ruler.

2 IN THE THICK OF THINGS

Missouri, 1884

I heard the crack of the whip and tried not to flinch even though I was fifty feet away. Cissy was getting punished again after trying to escape. The Redcoats didn't want to hang her. She and her sister Ida were two of the best workers in the field.

The sisters came from a long line of slaves. They weren't book smart, but they knew how to farm and keep a homestead. They were above average height, thick black girls, stronger than even men in the village, while still in their teens.

"Come on now Lavinia. Bring that water in for the soldiers. And I want to make a poultice for Cissy."

"But Mama, it's so heavy." I whined.

"You need to get stronger. The world will not get any easier."

"If I get it inside, will you tell me a story of when things were easier, Mama?"

My poor mother sighed. She looked older than her forties. Constant exposure to the sun and wind had wrinkled her skin. Anxiety had put silver streaks in her dark brown hair. "Yes Lavinia, tonight before bed. But you have to get chores done too."

"Yes Mama!" I was so excited by the prospect of a new

story that I hiked up the pail with both arms and ran it into the soldiers' quarters as fast as I could. I didn't even make a splash. I wouldn't realize until long afterward how important it was that I delivered the water.

Because of my sweet cherub looks and kind nature, I'd become a kind of mascot for the troops of our village. Despite the repeated violence and reminders of our slavery, I'd managed to filter out most of the bad things that happened around us.

The adults of the village noticed this and encouraged my parents to push me front and center at every task. I entertained the Redcoats with songs and dances I made up. In return, I'd get extra food, clothing or trinkets from them. I was told to listen to everything they said, then repeat it back to Papa, but only when Papa and I were alone. Papa would take my nuggets of information and feed it to a group, the Underground, which managed to survive the war. At ten years old, I was unknowingly one of their best spies.

I was rewarded from the village with an education because it would certainly make me a better interloper. I could see things, maps, drawings, journals, and joyfully tell Papa what I'd casually viewed from the interactions with the military.

The day that Cissy was whipped was one of the last I'd see my parents. After dark, Cissy came to our room.

"Cissy, you can't keep running if you don't think you can make it." My mother chided as she blended mustard seed, onion, and peculiar herbs and boiled them on our minute stove. We were lucky to have materials to cook with, another gift we received for my kindness to the Redcoats.

"I was so close, Missus James. Maybe a mile or two to the caves." Cissy wiped her almond shaped eyes that she inherited from her father who'd been killed after the war. Ida's eyes were different because her mom had found a new beau later on. That's how I kept the two apart, by the shape of their eyes. Rumor was that their parents got to the Underground. That's one reason why Cissy kept trying to run.

"Cissy, you girls need to be careful. Wait like the others. I don't think you'll be so lucky next time." Mama lifted the stinky mixture off the stove and added a pinch of spring water to it. "Lavinia, grab a rag."

"Yes, mama." I jumped up to grab a strip of well-worn cloth from the pantry. "Can I have another piece of bread?"

"No Lavinia, that's all we have for tomorrow. Now Cissy, pull up that shirt and let me see." She complied. My mother brought a dish with the home-made concoction over to our only table. "Oh Cissy."

"Is it bad?" I practically threw the rag at my Mama.

"Naw, just a few scratches." Cissy blew off the whipping. To me, it was terrible. Three long slashes on her back. Cissy hissed through her teeth as Mama applied the poultice and a rag.

"Does it hurt?" I was in Cissy's face with an odd smile. I loved having her around. After her parents disappeared, my mother helped her and Ida out. The Redcoats didn't offer them much of anything despite their hard work.

"Aw shucks, Lavinia, it ain't nothin'." I watched Cissy's knuckles turn white as Mama finished dressing the wounds.

"Lavinia, go to bed. I'll come tell you a story like I promised."

"But—" I protested. I wanted to read and talk to Cissy. She

and Ida were the closest thing I had to sisters in the village.

"No, bedtime. Now."

"Alright." I groaned. "Night, Cissy!" I pecked her on the cheek and plopped into the big bed I shared with my parents.

"Night, little Lavinia!" Cissy laughed.

I picked up a book and read. I let my mind go to the story about creatures in the woods. I was so entranced, that I didn't hear Cissy leave. Nor Mama cleaning up. I also didn't notice that Papa hadn't come home. I was shocked when Mama put her hand on the book.

"Don't you want to hear a real story?" Mama grinned.

"Yep!"

"Shhh. You know I have to whisper, right?"

"Yes Mama."

"Alright then." Mama slid in next to me and told me about how grandpa had been a farmer. He'd had lots of pigs that Mama played with. "One day, I liked one of the piglets so much that I dressed it up like a doll. Grandpa demanded I give it to him, that it wouldn't get too tame. The poor piglet got confused and with the coolness of grandpa's coat, he peed right down the front."

"Pee yew!" I giggled.

"Yes, smelly!" Mama smiled until there was a knock at the door. I will never forget the look on her face. I'd seen it multiple times before: before villagers were punished, when food ran out, but most scary of all, when Redcoats were looking for people.

The knock repeated. "Lavinia, go to sleep." She threw the

cover up and jumped off the bed.

"But Mama."

"Shhhh!" She put her finger to her lips. I had to be silent. I got scared and covered my face with my blanket. I couldn't understand why the Redcoats were nice to me but mean to everyone else.

I heard them at the door. They sounded pretty angry, but I couldn't hear who they would be searching for.

Mama used her sweetest voice to calm them down and they exited. I fell asleep to the usual rustling around our quarters.

"Lavinia, get up. We have to get to the fields early today." Mama shook me out of bed. It was still dark outside, and I could hear the plop of raindrops on the roof.

"But Mama, it's raining." I rubbed my eyes.

"No protests today, Lavinia. We have to get going. There's still work to be done." I got dressed as Mama put a couple of bundles under the bed. "You can have warm milk if you hurry." She coaxed.

I scurried to get my well-worn boots on while Mama braided my hair. As soon as she was finished, she plucked the last piece of bread out of the cupboard and put it in a shallow bowl with a remainder of the milk. "Now listen, there's a lot to be done today. But when we're finished, I want you home for supper. Don't lollygag or stop to chat with Cissy or Ida. I need you here to help."

"Okay Mama." I slurped up the meager breakfast as she hauled out coats. "Remember, home for dinner?"

"Yes Mama." I buttoned my threadbare woolen jacket and followed her out the door.

It was still early spring, and the cold drops of rain kept me awake as we scurried to the fields. Mama had brought a satchel and put it aside as we prepared to help with planting.

Papa soon joined us. Even in the wet dawn, I could tell he was more tired than usual. My parents whispered as we put out tools for the others and my father wolfed down bread that Mama had brought.

With a sloshing of mud, two Redcoats came aside us. At nighttime they were especially scary. The tips of the gun barrels glowed green with mini lights.

"Ah Mr. James, you were gone all night. Perhaps we could speak to you about it?" They pretended to be civil, but they shoved my father behind the tool shed before he could even answer.

Mama grabbed my hand. "It's time to use the outhouse."

"But I don't have to potty." I wondered what Papa was doing with the Redcoats.

"Yes, you do Lavinia." She dragged me into the stinky shed and tears burned my eyes as I desperately tried to pee.

"I'm trying Mama." I thought she was upset at me.

"It's alright Lavinia. Just try to finish." She wiped her face on her sleeve with a hiccup. "You don't have to hurry." Later on, I would realize that bathrooms could be both the worst and best places to hide.

I was finally able to pass some urine by thinking hard about the rain. My Mama peered through the slats of the wooden lavatory. I heard the Redcoats laugh and then ride away.

"Let's go Lavinia." Mama's voice trembled. I had never gotten off the pit that fast before. She burst through the door to Papa.

He stumbled and crashed into the rows of mud, groaning and grasping at his side. My Mama fell to her knees next to him, the slop splattering her dress. I heard them whisper frantically as Mama wiped his face clean. Eventually she was able to help him get up and moved to a worktable next to the shed.

"Come here Lavinia." The raspy sound of his voice scared me so much that I was stuck in the outhouse doorway. I'd never seen Papa like that. His face writhed in pain as Mama bandaged him up. "Come on, don't be scared." He puffed through clenched teeth as I finally moved towards them.

"Papa, are you hurt?" I trembled.

"Just a little, pumpkin. Don't you fret." His breathing slowed and he sipped water from a tiny canteen Mama had hidden under her dress.

"You rest, at least until the others get here." Mama ordered Papa and then turned to me with ferocity glowing in her eyes. "Lavinia, you don't say anything about this to anyone. Not the other slaves, not Cissy or Ida, and absolutely nothing to the Redcoats, no matter what they offer you. Understood?"

"Yes, Mama."

"Good then. Get the tools lined up for the others. They should be coming soon." Mama stroked Papa's face and I warmed inside. I was lucky to have two parents. I knew lots of children from the village that didn't even have one.

As workers arrived, they noticed my father's appearance but said nothing for fear of reprisal. It was eerily silent with a steady light rain wetting our skin. The occasional soldiers would check on our progress, with the splashing of the horse hooves trotting around the muddied fields. Soon it was apparent that the rain wasn't going to let up and the slaves were sent to other tasks. Mama and Papa stayed to clean up and bade me to entertain the soldiers. "Go along Lavinia." Mama showed me a thin smile while rain ran down her bonnet and escaped onto her cheeks. I didn't remember much of the rest of the afternoon, but I will always wonder if those drops had been tears.

"Lavinia, stay down!" Cissy hissed through clenched teeth. I was hiding with her and Ida in a briar patch.

My skin was crawling with pricks and scratches from the briars and mosquito bites. I could barely stand the pain and kept bobbing in the mud. I wanted my Mama. All hell had broken loose since I missed dinner two hours ago.

Time had escaped me. I had gone to the soldiers' mess hall to sing and dance for the men. They were grateful to get out of the storm and started swilling copious amounts of liquor. I was rewarded with sweets and laughter from them.

These uneducated Redcoats were on the lowest rung of the military. Most of them would never get married. Some could satisfy their needs with prostitutes with short trips to the nearest city, St. Louis. Fraternizing with village women was reserved for higher ranks. They were given decent quarters and good meals, but most led lives of bullying and unfortunately, rounding up escaped workers for execution.

For a young girl like me to sing to them was a small piece of heaven. After the beginning of the day had been horrific, I was more than happy to sing the old folk songs to a captive audience. This was the last time I would be that precocious. I'd completely forgotten that Mama had told me to be home for dinner. A gong rang out as the village was filled with screams. One of the village homes was engulfed in flames.

The drunken troop grabbed their weapons and headed for the streets. I ran out behind them in confusion. Then remembered I should've been home. The clock tower in the village square chimed out seven times.

I ran to our room calling out, "Mama! Papa!" When they weren't there, I had sunk to the floor in agony. I hadn't listened to Mama. I didn't know where to go.

"Lavinia! Come on!" Cissy ran into the room and scooped me off the floor.

"Where's Mama?" I screamed and she dropped me.

"Hush! Run this way." She grabbed my hand and pulled me past the outside perimeter of the village where Ida joined us. We headed for the fields when we heard the clomping of horses.

"Down the hill, through the forest!" Cissy barked. We slid through the wet grasses and under a maze of trees until we crashed into the briar patch.

Back in the village, workers ran everywhere, putting out the fire, gathering others to help, yet still others tried to escape. We could hear their screams as some were shot in the fields while others succumbed to the flames.

Redcoats passed us at times, their lighted bayonets sending shivers down our spines. We trembled in the dark until the sounds of the blaze stopped, and calm was restored.

"Now listen, we gonna go back to the village all quiet like. If anyone asks where we'd been, we were helpin' put out the fire on the other side. Let me talk, don't y'all say nothin'. Understood?" Cissy stood and checked around. She had managed to drag a lamp along and lit it after a deep sigh. She touched my shoulder. "Lavinia, you gotta pretend nothin' is wrong. You don't know nothin' and you can't be scared."

I nodded. I didn't know what else to do. We crept up from the bottom of the hill. We could hear the clatter of hooves and hysterical voices as we approached the village. Workers splashed buckets of spring water on the last of the embers. About a third of the village had burned. We slipped into the crowd unnoticed and helped with the clean-up.

Redcoats were dragging the dead away while others questioned the slaves.

As we toiled away long into the night, the others whispered about what truly happened. Days later, Cissy and Ida would explain to me that my parents escaped with a group called the Underground. One of the workers with them got scared and kicked over a lamp near a storage tent which started the fire. Chaos had ensued.

All through the night the remaining workers gossiped, but all I could hear was, "I can't believe they'd leave her behind." I would never see my parents again.

3 OTHER THINGS OF NOTE

The Kingdom had a basic set of strict rules that was followed worldwide. The rules were posted everywhere that mattered: schools, governing buildings, and ironically, places of worship, because loyalists were to honor their Queen above all. The largest displays were in town squares. Some were embraced by angels or sculptural representations of her majesty. They were the greatest reminder of adherence to the laws, for any capital punishment was executed quite publicly in those spaces.

I remember the first time I saw a death in the center of the village. We had to walk two miles from the farm where we had to work that day in order to get into town. I was five years old, and my legs ached from the early morning hike. My father was to return to the fields immediately after the noon time. For my very pregnant mother, carrying me wasn't an option. But we had to be there. It was law.

The town crier approached a hefty wooden platform. He cleared his throat to address the crowd. "Hear ye, hear ye. By her Majesty's law, this man, known as Marcus, is guilty of treason for trying to escape work camp. Per her Majesty's law, punishment is hanging. Bring the prisoner forward." The crier commanded two men who wore black hooded robes.

"Mommy—" I worried aloud. The tension of the crowd grew. Fear gripped me as I clung to her.

"Shhh. Don't you say another word." My mother bent down and hissed in my ear.

A young black man was hustled forward. His hands were bound behind him. One eye was swollen. His thin linen clothing was ripped and splattered with blood. It was clear that he'd been beaten to set an example.

"Tie!" The crier shouted. The executioners put a thick rope around the prisoner's neck then fastened it to a large t-shaped pole.

"Place!" The crier called out again. The prisoner was pushed onto a specific spot. He stumbled and nearly fell. "Control him, you idiots!" Redcoats were amongst us in the crowd, and they laughed at the poor soul that was about to die.

The crier continued. "You are sentenced to hang; may God have mercy on your soul."

And with those words, one of the hooded men pushed a lever and part of the platform dropped out beneath the escapee. The force from the rope tightening was strong enough that the prisoner's tongue sprout from his mouth and his good eye popped from his socket. It rolled down off the platform and landed on the ground next to me. I screeched into my mother's skirt.

A Redcoat picked up the errant orb and laughed. "A memento anyone? Anyone."

"That's enough now." The crier bellowed. "You can go home. But you can never leave." More bizarre laughter echoed amongst the soldiers.

A voice from above startled me. "Girl, look up at me." My mother hid her tears as she held my hand. "Follow the rules, Lavinia. Always."

I gazed up at the words that had been inscribed into massive grey tablets mounted behind the gallows. The rules were:

1. Honor Thy Queen and her sovereignty.

2. All work is done in honor of her Majesty.

3. All property belongs to the Kingdom.

4. All are to serve the Kingdom once of age.

5. All able-bodied males are to serve in her militia for a minimum of five years.

6. Any treason is grounds for execution.

7. Honorable service to her Majesty will be rewarded.

In my uneducated five-year-old mind, I hoped to be rewarded and not ever be guilty like the prisoner who was left listing in the wind for over a week in the square.

That night, my mother miscarried my only chance at a sibling. The long walk and the harsh display of violence was more than she could bear.

4 DISCOVERED

I was only fourteen when I first met Captain Davis. He ended four years of misery for me.

After my parents' disappearance, I was put in a room with Cissy and Ida. I was a liability. Nobody wanted to harbor a child that the parents could come back for. If caught doing anything related to escaping, punishment would certainly be death on the gallows.

The Redcoats never did find my parents, or the twenty others that escaped with them. Rumors had run rampant for years that there were caves on the riverbanks just south of the village and that they'd escaped there.

The soldiers thought I was purposely made into a decoy, although they couldn't prove that a ten-year-old could pull off such a feat. Besides, what kind of parents would leave such a smart beautiful child like me behind? My days as a pleasant distraction were over.

New troops were brought in with higher ranking officials, including a Colonel. The fields had given up good harvests over the last several years. This Colonel had wondered why it'd been ignored. He made a promise to the higher ups that it could bring in more profit. He wanted to make an impression in his new assignment, additional workers were brought in, and the village rebuilt. A glorious Victorian mansion was created, for the Colonel had a tempestuous and spoiled wife. Proper quarters were built for his troops. Higher ranked men had access to new homes, better food, new equipment, and ladies to entertain them.

Most of the new Redcoats had their own servants and additional slaves chosen to work for them. They recanted stories to the others of the plush furnishings and fancy clothing. The scraps leftover from savory meals were better than the slop that they'd eaten for years.

The Colonel instituted new harsh rules. The slaves weren't allowed to reproduce. A frightening order was posted in the village square within weeks of his arrival; there were too many children, too many mouths to feed. Food that could be fueling the Kindgom. Women and children's quarters were separated from the men. Once of a certain age, female and male adolescents were sent to live with their respective sexes. Anyone that resisted was whipped.

With large groups of new troops arriving, the soldiers wanted wives. Another decree was issued. Each May first, all females over the age of sixteen were to be lined up in the square. This was to be called the "Draw". Eligible officers, by order of rank, could choose their mate. If already espoused, they could pick from the "lesser" women for mistresses. Lots would be drawn for the standard field ranks to decide who had the next pick of the litter.

The first Draw was only six weeks after my parents and the others had escaped. That day will be burned in my mind forever. I was still in a room with Cissy and Ida, but Cissy had just turned seventeen. We barely had time to try to develop a plan.

"If I'm picked, I'll find a way to get food, supplies. I promise." Cissy gripped our hands tightly as we sat on the floor of our room that was barely big enough to hold our bed. "If I can find a way out, I will. We'll all get out." I'd already lost my parents; I was going to lose another family member. Ida and I simultaneously burst into tears. "Now hush you two. We'll make it work somehow. Remember, not a word about the caves to anyone."

We held on to each other as rapid, pounding knocks echoed through the village. Shouts and screams soon followed.

Redcoats emptied out all the quarters. The male slaves had already been sent to the fields to work. There had been a slim hope that they might continue to at least see their kin during daylight hours. With the roundup of all the women, all hope was lost.

Ida screamed when a Redcoat rapped on our door. Cissy admonished her. "Stop it. You'll only make it worse." Tears fell over Cissy's cheeks. It was the first time I'd ever seen her cry. "Just stop it. You have to be brave. Tell me you will be."

Before Ida could answer, two Redcoats came in. "Let's go. Don't make it hard." The older one, a Sargent by his stripes, grimaced through a salt and pepper beard as he reached for me on the floor. Cissy wiped her eyes and slapped his hand away in one smooth stroke.

"I'll help them up." She pouted angrily.

"Come on now, don't dawdle. You touch me like that again missy, you may not be alive to be selected." The Sargent huffed.

The younger one snorted at Cissy and I disliked him instantly. He had a swath of rusty hair that nearly pushed his cap off. One eye was grey and the other green. I could feel the discomfort in my belly as his eyes raked over me.

Cissy remained still as she helped us scramble through the door, our oppressors not far behind.

We joined tens of other women and children in the street on a regrettable march to the square. I'd never seen so many fearful faces. Not even on the night of the fire.

The obviously older women were already lined up in front of the gallows when we arrived. Within a few more minutes, the remaining ladies shuffled in nervously to join our doomed crew.

"Attention!" The bearded Sargent yelled. "We will start by the honor system first. If any of you are sixteen or older, you must come forward and stand with the others."

The older women came forward, guessing correctly that their wrinkles and streaks of grey would betray them anyway. After the sergeant cleared his throat, about twenty more crossed the street to line up after giving last tearful hugs to their families.

Cissy hesitated, hoping that the Redcoats wouldn't notice that she was taller than most of us that remained. The sergeant again cleared his throat and flicked on the light on his bayonet. I watched Cissy as she exhaled and crossed the road with yet another group of resisters. "No, Cissy." Ida moaned and dropped to her knees. I joined her on the ground and tried to comfort her.

"Silence!" The Sergeant grumbled. "You have one more minute to cross. Then I will start calling out names. If you are on the wrong side, you will be punished."

Several more scurried over. The younger red-haired soldier glared at me. I was eleven now. I wasn't going to move. Suddenly it was silent. You could hear the robins chirping in the forest on the other side of the village. The minute passed.

"Alright then ladies. It's time for roll call. Then we will begin the selection process. I will call your name, you will repeat your name and your age, no matter what side you're on. Again, if you are on the wrong side, you will be punished. This is your last chance." His eyes bore holes into the women around him.

One last woman handed off her baby to another adolescent girl and went over. She hid her face in her worn-out sweater, but everyone could hear her sobs. The baby also cried.

"Take that infant to the quarters and shut it up, or I'll do it." The Sergeant had lost his patience. The Redcoats snickered. The teen with the baby ran off towards one of the housing units.

"Now then, we'll proceed. This has taken far too long." The Sargent rapidly called out the names. Anyone that mumbled or took too long to answer was verbally admonished. We trembled as he flew through the list.

I helped Ida off the ground as her name was called. "Ida Clark, fifteen." She spoke loud and clear.

The Sergeant smirked. "Lavinia James."

"I'm Lavinia, eleven." Chills spilled over me. The younger soldier's eyes bore right through me. Ida saw it too.

"Thank God you're too young Lavinia." She barely whispered.

Soon nearly everyone's name had been called. There was one girl of mixed race that stood apart from the others. She gazed at the forest and fidgeted with the edges of her dress sleeves. I thought for sure she was the same age as Cissy. Her name was called.

"Gertrude Perkins." The sergeant barked.

Gertrude stopped moving. Everyone quivered and looked around for an agonizing moment. Most eyes settled on her. The silence was horrifying.

The sergeant scanned both sides of the street. "Gertrude Perkins?" He raised his voice yet higher.

Gertrude bolted, her long braids flying behind her. "Private!" The sergeant hollered. The young soldier that had terrified me, brought a whip from under his coat. He ran after her, cracking his weapon. He struck her at least three times, but she didn't stop.

We watched in horror as he got close enough to send the whip around her neck and drag her into the mud.

"I won't go. I won't go." She sputtered as he tugged harder. Her face reddened.

"Private!" The sergeant called out.

The Private released the whip and Gertrude plopped face down in the muck. As he prepared to take further orders, she pushed up to run. In a split second, the Private lunged with his bayonet and gored Gertrude with a hissing electrified blade. We clung to each other, screamed, and cried at her demise.

"Get her out of here!" His superior ordered. "Silence."

The Private grabbed Gertrude's lifeless body by her dress collar and dragged her back in front of us in a grim parade before taking her behind the gallows. "She was half and half anyway." The Private mumbled to the group of waiting soldiers that salivated over the eligible ladies.

The Sergeant called out the last two names and the roll call was finally finished. There was no time for goodbyes, for he grabbed one of the younger women on the over sixteen side. "You're mine. Go sit over there on step to the gallows." The

Sergeant's new unwilling fiancé whimpered while running to the step.

"Attention! Men, assemble in rank order and make your selections. Do it now, your brothers in arms have been waiting far too long."

So it began, the men choosing. Some were quick, having already seen what they liked. Others touched the women's hair, faces, or breasts through their clothing, before deciding. I was forever sickened by their behavior. In my heart, I swore I would never let them take me.

Finally, it was over. Each of the soldiers slipped away with their respective picks. Three women remained. One was Cissy. The Sergeant growled at them. "Go on back with the others."

We jumped for joy at our blessing, until the Sergeant spoke again. "Get back to your quarters. Tomorrow, we start fresh." The way he glared at us started a new worry in my gut.

"Damn, that was close." Cissy smiled and hugged us as we went back to our room. A Redcoat was waiting there. "Get your things and go to building number three. Don't take too long." He scribbled on a piece of paper and waited for us. Not until we were well on our way with the others, did he finally leave his post. As we walked Cissy reminded us, "Remember, no matter how close or well we think we know the others, ain't nobody is to know about the caves."

With barely time to recover from the morning's drama, we were moved into the new halls. Gone were our old rooms. We now were housed in dormitories made up of long and nondescript buildings. We were put into teams by our talents. Cissy, Ida, and I remained farmers. We were just one rung up from the bottom on the hierarchy of slaves. Even the women that were chosen during the Draw had to take on group assignments in addition to their nighttime duties. I remember just being grateful that I wasn't on outhouse detail.

That first year in the refurbished village was brutal. The oldest women became nannies to the youngest. Although it sounds like this was a good idea, most of these children never saw their parents again. Once they got old enough to do any kind of task, they were put to work. Preteens and adolescents under sixteen worked in their groups with their elders.

At night, after lights out, girls cried in their bunks. The very first night after the Draw no one slept.

We were poor before, but now it was a kind of organized hell. Only the Redcoats and their families had access to fun or entertainment. I used to hear about what larger cities were like and what people did. The new Redcoats cut us completely off from the outside world.

Groups became further divided and cliques developed. Girls who worked directly with Redcoat families stopped talking to the others. We used to share everything. Even in the most desperate times, we were family. Now we only knew our work.

But you could tell what we did by our scars. Cooks had burns and cuts. Seamstresses constantly rubbed their sore fingers. Some of them developed limps from pushing the machinery pedals with one foot. The latrine girls could never quite get rid of the odor they worked around. They got sick more than any other group. Maids had raw hands from constant cleaning. Cissy, Ida, and I had blisters that never went away and dry, sunburnt skin from hours in the fields. The older girls actually wanted to get picked during the next Draw, in the hopes they wouldn't have to work so hard.

We all became thin, our clothes almost falling off us. They

fed us the bare minimum to keep us working. I thought I was tired before. Now I knew the meaning of exhausted.

But the most frightening thing happened. Every once in a couple of months, one or two workers would disappear. Gone. Vanished. We had hoped they escaped, but I think most of us knew that they died. Weaker workers were sent to infirmary. Some never came back. They would be replaced when trains came in with fresh slaves. It might only be a two or three. Other times there were twenty or more. The Private that killed Gertrude was promoted to Lieutenant. He leered at me whenever he had the chance.

You could tell that the city girls had been brought for punishment. They had no idea how to live off the land and it showed. They soon were the thinnest and most bruised.

Again, I was blessed. I was taught at a young age what plants in the forest were safe to eat. We still managed to get off the field to steal berries or mint plants.

Winter was the worst. We had one stove for the large dormitory. It barely warmed a corner in the room. Most of us ended up dragging our blankets to the floor and sleeping in massive piles.

Spring brought anxiety and notification of the second Draw. The fields had been expanded. Once private farms had been industrialized by the Kingdom. Arriving trains had brought in less women and more troops as of late. And for the first time, the soldiers were of mixed races. Our land was now the most prized soil in the world.

On the morning of May first, the bunk hall was full of panicked whispers and crying. Several girls purposely tried to dress poorly by not cleaning up or wearing work clothes from the day before. Others hated their jobs so much, that they'd stolen old or worn-out dresses from soldiers' wives or paramours to make a better impression. They fixed their hair with such passion it made the younger girls squirm with both fear and envy.

Cissy braided my hair while Ida braided hers. Cissy tried to prepare us. "Now just be calm. Don't cause a fuss. Tell the truth."

We again lined up at the gallows. I was now twelve and it was obvious that my transition into womanhood had begun.

Cissy was chosen to be a mistress by a black soldier. Ida was selected by one of lesser Redcoats. I didn't know a whole lot about men, only that once that I started what they called "bleeding time", that I could get pregnant. I prayed that Cissy and Ida would endure whatever fate threw at them. The Lieutenant picked a wife, which surprised everyone.

The next two years were incredibly lonely. I'd only see Ida on days she'd work in the field. The third Draw was only a terrifying reminder that I could be picked in a matter of a couple of years. The Lieutenant had selected a mistress. I hoped to God I'd never be selected by him.

We had a mild winter which again expanded the scope of the farms. Fields further west grew squash, carrots, beets, and cabbage. Even further, grapes were harvested for wine. The abundance of our region reached the upper ranks of the Kingdom. Again, more troops and workers arrived with the spring.

The Colonel was seen less as of late. A rumor made the rounds that he'd been ill. Which meant the Lieutenant came to observe more often. He continued to let his eyes linger on me. At fourteen, I was growing into adolescence. Redcoats that worked the field stared at me. Other girls whispered behind my back. I finally got a chance to catch up with Ida to ask. "Why are people talking, staring? What's all the fuss about?"

"Lord, girl. God blessed you to be pretty. I was goin' to say something four months ago at harvest 'cause I ain't seen you in a while. Your hair is gettin' thick and long. You got a chest men want to touch." Ida scanned the field then continued to work beside me. "Girls are still disappearing, the prettiest ones. And I don't think all of them are runnin'. Lavinia, you need to watch. All the time. Don't get too close to anybody 'cause I hear the other girls are snitching. Keep to yourself and don't make a fuss."

I bent down and continued to pull stalks from the ground. My head hurt from trying to hold back tears.

"Now don't be cryin', Lavinia. You might get lucky. Cissy's mister is good to her. She's getting' extra food now and a good bed. Me too. I still gots to work, but at night, I get more time to sleep, especially if my man is with his wife." I shuddered at the thought of being chattel. "Ain't no shame in it. And you is book smart, you always speak like the English. An' you sing too. I reckon you git a good one picking you."

"I guess you're right."

"You know I am." Ida embraced me. For a moment I hoped she was correct.

On a cool spring morning, we were sent to the fields to prepare the ground for seeding. Odd new machines had been brought in. Strange contraptions that pulled the plows with the strength of two horses. They blew off billows of hot steam and black smoke that dirtied the bright blue skies.

They'd brought in more Redcoats and male slaves to run the machines. I tried to ignore their stares as I worked with a group to clean up the furrows that the mechanical monsters had made.

There was an abrupt call to halt operations. A group of new

Redcoats strolled in from a carriage. Soldiers dismounted from the vehicles and stood at attention. "Girls! Stand!" The Lieutenant barked.

I wiped my sweaty face with an old handkerchief and tucked it into my apron. I stood silently with my hoe as a higher ranked soldier approached with two assistants.

"Captain, welcome to the fields." The Lieutenant greeted in the nicest tone I'd ever heard him utter.

"So, this is where the best food is coming from?" His genteel accent was not from the former Americas. The Captain was impeccably dressed, more like a gentleman than a soldier. He removed his top hat to reveal short well-trimmed black locks. He put a leather gloved hand to cover his deep brown eyes as they scanned the fields in the bright spring sunshine.

"Yes, Sir. The absolute best." The Lieutenant faked a smile as we continued to listen.

"And the machines? Working well as planned?"

"Ah yes, Sir. Going through the dirt like silk."

"Very well then." The Captain slapped on his hat and addressed the workers. "Carry on then!"

I had been too hot from the hard work. I whisked off my bonnet to cool my head. It was freeing to let my hair loose for a moment. I completely forgot my surroundings, smiled, and inhaled the fresh air. My pause was interrupted by a rustling of the higher ranks.

"You, there! Miss1" Everyone stilled again. I tried to calm as I realized every single pair of eyes in the field were on me. The Captain called again. "Come forward. The rest of you, get back to work."

I glanced at Ida for a split second. She grimaced and went back to running a rake through chunks of rich earth. "Yes, Sir." I managed to speak even though my head was heavy. I lifted my skirts while walking towards the new official. I stood before him and fumbled a kind of curtsy that I remembered from my "entertaining the troops" days as a child.

"What is your name, Miss?" The Captain's eyes raked over me, but he didn't seem upset.

"I'm Lavinia, Sir."

"And your working group?" He questioned with a slight tilt of his chin.

"Farming, Sir."

"Have you always been farming?" His eyes narrowed. He made a motion for the other Redcoats to continue work. The Lieutenant curled his lip and walked away with the others.

"Yes, Sir." I realized I was still holding my bonnet and prepare to tie it back on.

"Hmm, come this way. You can leave your bonnet off." He walked towards the tool shed where a table and two chairs awaited us. "Sit."

My heart was pounding in my ears as he called for one of the soldiers. "Bring water." He again removed his hat and placed it on the table with a smoothness I'd never seen.

I nervously rubbed my hands over my persistent blisters and callouses.

"You're not in trouble Lavinia. I want to ask you a few

questions." Water was given to us in tin cups. A scowl covered the face of the Captain. "Tell me about farming here. How did you learn how to do it?" He brought the cup to his lips in a gingerly fashion.

"Well, um, my parents taught me how. They knew how to pick the right seed, when to plant, when to harvest. All by the seasons." I paused to drink and prayed I'd given him the right answers.

"Where are your parents?"

I gulped and tried not to spit out my water. "They disappeared, Sir."

"Hmmm. Do you know where?"

I shook my head. "They were gone after a fire one night."

He paused and stared into my eyes. "Just gone?"

"Yes, Sir, that's all I know." For some reason, that night came back to me, and I could not hold back the tears that betrayed me. I would find out later that this emotional outburst actually protected me.

"I am sorry about that Lavinia. It must've have been hard."

I had no idea how to respond. I nodded and tasted more of the fresh water.

The Captain leaned back in his chair. "And do you do other things?"

"Yes, Sir. Well, I mean, I used to, before the new Colonel came. I cooked, sewed, cleaned, traded things. I read and wrote. I even used to sing for the Redcoats." The words bubbled forth and, in my head, I chastised myself for giving away too much.

"Very good. Well, then, keep up the good work. But know that you may change groups very soon, Lavinia. We have other work in the Kingdom that you are better suited for." He stood and came over to my seat and pulled it out for me. I felt completely out of place and wondered if the others were watching.

His breath tickled my ear. "I have things for you to do, Lavinia. You are to tell no one. Don't step out of line or you'll die. Understand?"

My stomach ached as he backed away to allow me to stand. I trotted back to the planting. I heard the rustle of the other soldiers join him. The voice of the Lieutenant echoed in my brain.

"That one is trouble, Sir. Her parents escaped years back. You're going to want to keep an eye on her."

I struggled to focus on working, but I peered from under my bonnet. The Captain got one last good look at me from over his shoulder as they walked away.

London

Thousands of miles away, close to the world capital of London, a group linked to the Underground was digging tunnels and caves on a discreet bluff of the Thames. There was one particularly loose patch of earth that easily broke away in the crews' shovels. Then they froze. They hit something hard.

In fear of explosives or worse, they called a leader over. They cleared off the box that was clearly in the shape of a coffin. Embossed on the surface was a crown with pricey gold ink. The men gazed at each other in amazement. I would find out much later on, once deeply imbedded into the Underground, that these men had found the real body of our former Queen Victoria.

5 HOW TO SPEAK ENGLISH

A few months after that day when I first met my Captain in the field, it was time for the Draw.

The Captain came down to the fields at least once a day to check on progress. Every couple days, he would pull me aside to ask me specifics about the seeds and methods, right down to the size of the worms we found in the ground. He soon had me making notes and drawings in a thick bound book that he carried everywhere.

Cissy and Ida had been Drawn already and were getting along with their mates, although Cissy was moved from farming to another group. For the first time in a while, I didn't worry. I was fourteen. I wouldn't be selected for two more years.

The day before the Draw had begun like any other. We worked in the fields all day, some trying to make a good impression, others not caring because they weren't old enough to be taken.

The Captain came down late that afternoon. There were whispers that the Colonel was ill. His wife had passed from the same disease that he now suffered from. Word was that a new replacement Colonel was already in route. The Captain was busy preparing for his arrival. A furrowed brow and angry orders greeted most that he spoke with.

At the ring of the dinner bell, we scurried to put up tools and bags of seed. As I put the last of my tools away, the Captain whispered next to me. I jumped at his intrusion.

"Lavinia, I need you to stay and refresh the horses. I couldn't keep the older girls because they could be chosen tomorrow. I want them to have a good last evening here."

My mouth fell open. "Yes, yes, Sir."

"They're already in stables with hay. Just refill the water bins. If there's no food left when you get to the mess hall, come see me and I'll make sure you get fed. Understood?"

"Yes, Sir." Again, I bowed to him in my usual awkward fashion and ran for the new stables.

It was a brilliant red barn with plenty of room for twelve horses. It and a new machinery garage were near the old tool shed. Both buildings had been created with the Captain's initiative.

I lifted the latch and was warmed by the sunset that poured in through the windows as the fine steeds munched on fresh greens. They were magnificent beasts. The Captain had brought most of them here too.

A growl from my stomach reminded me that I should hurry. I pumped water as quick as my arm could move. The horses were grateful for the cool liquid. I patted each one as I finished. As I prepared to leave, the shadow of a man stood in the doorway.

"They're pretty. Fast too. Would help you make a quick exit, wouldn't they?" The bold eyes of the Lieutenant locked onto mine.

"I'm only leaving for dinner, Sir." I tucked loose tendrils under my bonnet while trying to think of a way to pass him.

"Really? Is that what you were doing here? Getting ready for dinner?"

"The Captain asked me to. Sir." I was trembling at this point, barely able to keep my hands steady.

"You'd do anything he'd say wouldn't you? You're pretty good at taking orders." He went inside, while closing the door behind him, and set the latch. The Lieutenant grabbed a whip from his belt. Whinnies came up from the horses as they sensed my anxiety. "You know, with a new Colonel coming, and me catching someone like you trying to escape, well, I could be up for a big promotion. Word is that the Captain's work is soon done here anyhow." With each step he took towards me, my heart pounded more loudly in my ears. I stood back and held onto one of the stalls.

"But you know, we could make an arrangement to spare you. Say a little something now, a little something later, like tomorrow, when I choose you in the Draw."

I slid to the floor as he towered over me. As he reached at my bonnet, the barn door flew open.

"Lieutenant! Report to the mess hall now. That's an order." The Captain reached for his pistol as the Lieutenant swirled around.

I saw my chance, scrambled from the floor, and ran to the Captain's side.

"Now, Lieutenant!" The Captain pushed me behind him.

"Yes, Sir, Captain." The words slid clumsily out of his mouth. "On my merry way." The Lieutenant tipped his cap as he slid past us. "See you at the Draw tomorrow!"

A chill went through me as I prepared to follow him to the mess hall. "No Lavinia, come back inside."

He shut the door behind us, put down a blanket, and spread-out food from his satchel. "Sit down, Lavinia. I need you to eat in a hurry. I can't show any favoritism."

I couldn't believe the fantastic taste of the two slices of bread, a piece of roasted chicken, and an apple tart I was presented with. I almost ate it whole. The Captain set down his canteen. "You can wash it down with this." I responded with quick swills.

I watched him pace around the barn and then peer out the windows with a strange look on his face. He heard me cap off the canteen. "Finished?"

"Yes, Sir." The Captain helped me from the floor, and we folded the blanket. For the first time since before my parents escaped, I was cared for. My heart warmed when he touched my hand.

"Remember what I told you before, Lavinia. You can never say anything to anyone. It could kill you. You will hurry up to the dormitories and I will see you tomorrow. You are very valuable to the Kingdom. Be safe."

"Yes, Sir." I dashed to the dormitories just as the other girls came out of the mess hall. My timing was perfect. No one knew I was missing. At least that's what I thought.

The next morning, we lined up in the street, and tried to relax before the Draw. It was a brilliant sunny day. There weren't many women on the other side, probably less than ten. During roll call, two more ladies caved to their age and crossed over. A light wind blew through the village as the Sergeant read over his list. He whispered to other higher ranked soldiers. I noticed that the new Captain was not amongst the troops.

"Well, ladies, this year we have a problem. We have over twenty men that need brides, companionship. It is for the honor of the Kingdom to provide our soldiers, our men that protect us, with the most comfort we can provide. Therefore, the Colonel, has given me authorization to lower the eligibility age to what I see fit. We will start with fifteen." There were audible gasps. "Silence. During roll call there were at least three on the other side that were fifteen years of age. You must come forward now."

Four adolescents crossed the street in a hurry. I exhaled a sigh of relief. The Sergeant again perused his list. Soon all my hopes for a quick Draw were dashed. "Quiet everyone. Again, we are still too short on ladies for our soldiers. Therefore, I am authorized to again lower the age as I see fit. Fourteen is the new age. Anyone fourteen and over must cross over now."

As the Lieutenant smiled at me, I wanted to pass out. The sunlight blinded me, and I grabbed the sleeve of the girl next to me. I was held up by one of my coworkers. "C'mon Lavinia." It was a girl I talked to when Cissy and Ida were on house duties. She practically dragged me across the street to join the eligible females. I held on to her and tried to breathe. Not only was I not ready, I was absolutely frightened to my core. I heard the Sergeant call a more names, and the last group of unwilling girls joined us. I finally was able to stand, only to see the Lieutenant salaciously licking his lips.

I wanted to vomit. I wanted to die because I knew that he was now the highest ranked soldier after the Sergeant. He would choose me, and I would suffer the rest of my life. I glanced down at my beat-up boots.

"Now then, we will begin our Draw. Attention!" The troops got in line. "The Drawing begins now." I tried not to cry. I thought about running. A scuffle in the ranks forced me to look up.

"Looks like I made it just in time." I heard the pleasant lilt of my Captain cause his fellow soldiers to laugh.

"And who is your choice, Captain?" The Sergeant smirked.

"Lavinia James." He smirked at me.

I fainted.

"Lavinia, are you okay?" I blinked and tried to sit up.

"I-I..." Words fell out of my mouth as the Captain helped me come to. I gazed around an unfamiliar room. There were furnishings in well-crafted wood and vivid colors. The blankets I was wrapped in were incredibly plush.

"You're dehydrated. And still malnourished. I want you to eat and go back to sleep. Micah will help you until I come back." I thought he kissed my cheek as he left the room. A black man came into focus as he loomed over me.

"Miss Lavinia, I'm Micah. Here, drink." He held a glass to my lips. I sipped. It tasted so good that I was soon slurping and finished the glass. "Slow down. There's plenty more where that came from." His voice had the same pleasant accent as the Captain's. He refilled the glass with a pitcher from the nightstand. "Take your time." He smiled a toothy grin.

For the first time in my life, I had unlimited water. And everything else. "I have soup for you too. Leave room for food." He laughed as he placed a dinner tray over my lap.

An elegant place setting of rose painted china greeted me. Shiny silverware, a glass of milk, biscuits, and a cup of tea sat next to the bowl.

"Oh." I'd never seen such fancy tableware up close.

"Let me show you how to use all this." Micah briefly instructed me on table etiquette as I cleared off the plate. "My, you were hungry." He had a kind, subtle laugh.

"Where am I?" I finally spoke up.

"The Captain's house. This will be your room."

"The whole room?" I wondered aloud.

"Yes. You will have more things soon. And more answers to your questions. But you need to rest, Lavinia. Don't worry, I'll be here if you need anything."

I closed my eyes to sleep. Suddenly I had to run back to the barn, the Lieutenant close behind. My chest heaved as I bolted and then fell headlong into a pile of hay.

The Lieutenant was on me, his hot breath burning on my neck. "You're mine bitch! You cannot escape." His fingers held my chin and then reached down. He ripped open my blouse as I squirmed. As he grabbed for my breast, I screamed.

"Miss Lavinia!" Micha was at my bedside. It was dark outside and gas lamps bathed the room in a golden glow. "It's alright. Take deep breaths, you had a night terror."

He got me upright in a warm embrace. It was the safest I'd felt in a while.

"Now, now, water." He again prepared a glass for me, and I slugged it down greedily. "Aw darling, take your time. You're going to be fine."

I finally was calm. I closed my eyes for a moment and then opened them again to make sure that I was truly awake this time.

"I'll get Captain—" Before he finished, the Captain was running into the room.

"Lavinia, everything alright?" He pulled off his coat, threw it on a chaise, and sat on the bed. My mouth fell open at the sight of his deep brown eyes. "Nightmare?"

"Yes, yes." I stuttered.

"You're safe here. I won't let anyone harm you." He brushed his hand across my forehead. "You're a little warm. I'll call up the doctor to check on you. Then supper?"

"Yes. But—" I persisted.

"I want you not to think of anything else but rest for now. There will be plenty of things to learn later." He ordered me gently.

"Can I use the outhouse?" I pleaded as my bladder cramped like snakes sliding in my gut.

The Captain burst into laughter. "Well, no, but you can use the water closet." My confusion must have shown on my face for he had Micah lead me to the bathroom. The new servant showed me how to use the toilet. There were even soft cloths for wiping. I was alone to do my business.

Why was I bleeding? I rewiped. Again, spots of blood. I wasn't sure if this was womanhood, or I was very sick. I now wanted to see the doctor. I bunched up two of the cloths, stuffed them into the nicest pantaloons I'd ever worn, and tip toed to the bed. I still was possessed like I was living in a bizarre dream.

My timing was perfect. The doctor sure was fast enough. He was entering the room with the Captain by the time Micah had me tucked back in.

"Lavinia, this is Dr. Gideon. Do not hesitate to tell him anything about how you're feeling. I'll leave you with him for a moment and then we'll go from there. Don't be afraid." The Captain soothed as he and Micah exited.

As soon as the door shut, the doctor tried to speak. I cut to the quick.

"I think I've started, um, I think it's called, um, menses?"

I strained to hear the muffled conversation behind the bedroom door. I quashed my desire to run over and eavesdrop.

The doctor had just finished a thorough exam. I had never been so embarrassed in pulling down my bloomers. After quick prodding at my tummy, and him checking every orifice, he pronounced me healthy, considering that I'd never had enough to eat in my lifetime and still managed to start a menstrual cycle. He explained about my lady parts, to which I blushed throughout.

He had a bottle of tonic and gave me two sips. "I'm going to leave this behind. The Captain and Micah will know when to give you more. If you don't feel better in a day or two, you must tell the Captain. Understood, young lady?"

"Yes, Sir."

"Be well then Lavinia."

Their consultation was over. Micah came into the room with another tray of food. The Captain came to the bedside again.

Once the food was in place, Micah left without a sound.

"You need to eat again, even if you're not hungry. I'll talk while you eat."

"Yes, Sir." It wasn't hard to resist. There was soup and biscuits again. But this time, there was roasted chicken, greens, and sweet cream butter.

"I want you to know that you are safe here. Because of how things transpired today, that we will eventually be truly espoused."

My mouth fell open as he grinned ear to ear from my reaction.

"Keep eating, there's no hurry. We will have a formal ceremony in about a week. I have no desire for a mistress. I also do not rape young girls. However, that brings me to why I was late to the Draw today." He paused and then touched my hand. "You will never have to worry about the Lieutenant again. He was arrested and hanged today."

"What happened?" I tried to talk with my mouth full.

"After you left, I knew he hadn't truly gone back to quarters. Well, he may have gone for a brief moment, but I followed him as he headed for the forest. He went far out to the banks of the river. There was a cave he went to. All the missing girls and ladies were there."

"How did they all—" He interrupted with a sad look.

"He killed them, Lavinia. More than twenty."

I put my fork down.

"He was intending on taking you there, I'm certain. I've been watching him. And he certainly has been watching you. He was there quite a while. All night, it was, well, sickening, and I cannot tell you more. I had to inform the new Colonel. Your old master died last night as well and there was much activity around the house. That's why it took me so long to get to the Draw. The Lieutenant was arrested right after you fainted. The new Colonel was quite disturbed that workers were lost to his sickening desires."

"Mmm." My appetite was gone.

"I want you to stop worrying for now. Again, I need you to rest." He moved the tray away. "You're still very young Lavinia. I promise you this. I will not touch you until you are ready and only then if you want me to. Understood?"

"Yes, Sir." I flushed to my toes.

He grinned slyly. "When we are alone, you can call me Braden. That's my name." He paused and touched my face. "Tomorrow we'll try to have a normal day, learning about what you'll need to do around the house. Can I tuck you in?"

The prospect of being alone in such a big bed scared me. "Will you stay with me?"

A winsome look passed over his face and he sighed. "Yes, wait a moment and I'll be back."

I heard snippets of conversation with Micah and noises in the room next door. I was on the brink of falling back asleep when he entered the room.

He wore a long dressing gown covered by an impressive burgundy robe which he kept on.

"Now move over and make room." He smirked. "Here put this pillow between us, I don't want to crush you." He wrapped his arms around me and the pillows. "Good night, Lavinia."

"Good night, Captain." It didn't occur to me that I could call him by his first name.

"Don't talk that way in front of the Colonel." I was learning how to speak proper English from my Captain. "Remember start by lessening the stress on the t. Say button again."

"Button." I repeated.

"Try buh-hon." He encouraged.

"Buh-ton." I copied him.

"Much better. Remember, the goal is to start sounding like you came from the same place as I, which was London. You will be married to an officer; you need to sound proper." Braden was continuing with my lesson, when Micah entered the room with a note on fine crisp paper.

"Sorry to disturb you, Captain. I was told that you need to read it now."

Braden tore open the seal. He squinted at me over the immaculate message paper. "Micah, can you leave us, please?

"Yes, Sir."

As soon as Micah exited, my Captain began to question me. "Lavinia, did you know that Cissy escaped?"

I froze. In the time since the Draw, I'd been so busy

adjusting to my new life, I'd forgotten about everything else. But I never did forget that Cissy would do whatever needed to help us. And I knew she meant escaping. The Draw was the perfect distraction, there was no doubt in my mind that she was gone.

"No." I don't know how I managed to lie to a man that had both told me I could die and that he would protect me within the space of a few weeks. "She never said anything."

"Are you certain?" Braden raised his eyebrows and leaned in towards me.

"I don't remember anything." I tried to let my body go limp.

Cissy always said to relax if ever questioned. "Pretend you're a rag doll. Limp like." Her words echoed in my head.

"You know I am going to question Ida. Cissy put you both in danger. This is your last chance." His brown eyes bore into mine.

"I don't know. I am sorry. I wish I could help."

My Captain stood and glared at me. "Alright Lavinia. We'll discuss your punishment when I get back. That is, if I've found out you've lied to me. You can study while I'm gone." He ran from the room, yelling at Micah for his coat.

I rushed to the window. He was on his horse in seconds. I went back to the table and sipped my tea. Micah came in moments later.

"Miss Lavinia, would you like more tea?"

"Yes, Micah. Please." I tried to be demure as well as a farm girl thrown into an unknown world of crazy upscale violence could be.

He was precise in his pour. Micah did everything like that, from the way he dressed, to how he greeted people that came to the door. He then sat down in Braden's vacated seat.

"What's wrong, Miss Lavinia?"

"It's nothing. The Captain has serious business."

"You know that he cares very much for you. He knew that you'd be in trouble from day one of his arrival." To my amazement, Micah poured himself a cup. "I've been with him a long, long time, and I have never seen him so protective, so charmed by anyone, soooo quickly." His eyes lingered on mine as he drank. There was a long uncomfortable pause.

"I appreciate that, Micah. I really do." I pretended to look down at my studies.

"But you haven't been truthful though. You know that must hurt him. I mean, he's a Captain. He's seen a lot of things." His genteel needling continued.

"I told him everything I knew, Micah. Now, if you don't mind, I need to study." I only had to look him in the eye once, I thought. Make it good. I stared at him and didn't flinch.

"Um hmmm. Alright Miss Lavinia. You go on and study now then." He slipped out of the room.

I attempted to read for a while. I glanced over the same passage again and again, but nothing stuck in my head. I wondered where Cissy was. Did they catch her? And now were they going after Ida? Would Ida be tortured and hung like the others?

I went into the downstairs water closet and vomited my tea.

I let myself sob for a while. It felt like forever since I'd been able to cry. I'd been close to death so many times, I'd never know how I'd react anymore. I finally got off the floor and checked my dressings. My first menstrual cycle was over. Would I live to be a woman? Would I want to?

There was a tap on the door. "Miss Lavinia, are you alright? The Captain is on his way in."

"I'm coming, I was feeling unwell." I tried to sound calm. I fixed my hair as best I could and poured cool water from the basin over my eyes until my facial redness was gone. I purposely didn't hurry back to the library. I strolled back to my chair and poured more tea. If I was going to die, at least I would die sated, I reasoned. I looked over the same passage one more time as the Captain came in.

"Micah, bring in scones. And butter please." The Captain sat down. I absently wondered if the seat was still warm from Micah temporarily stealing it. "Lavinia, Micah says that you weren't well when I'd gone?"

"I'm still adjusting to the food, I would suppose." I was saddened to see Braden worn out. From the chimes of the clock in the library, he'd been gone less than an hour. That would've been plenty of time to question, arrest, or kill.

Micah brought in the scrumptious smelling food. "Thank you, Micah." He began to butter the scones. "You need to eat Lavinia. Be careful though, these knives can be, well, very, very sharp. Enough to cut through a finger."

"I'm not very hungry. May I rest?" I ignored the threat and prepared to stand.

"No, sit down. And listen." His tone darkened. "Lavinia, I

want you to always remember this. When I questioned Ida about Cissy's disappearance, Ida gave up the truth almost immediately. You, however, never broke. Keep that in mind, don't ever break."

I tried to ease back into my seat. "Why? What happened to Ida?" I was totally unprepared for this scenario and immensely confused.

"Nothing happened to Ida. Cissy escaped. I know because I helped her."

6 BELOW THE SURFACE

"It will get easier each time, I promise." Braden brushed my hair away from my face and rubbed an errant tear cross my cheek. "You need to be relaxed. Confident. Smile and be coy. Understand?" I mushed my face further into his chest as he reached round my ribs. "And we need to get you fattened up more." A cold rain poured outside our bedroom. It was glorious to be tucked into a warm bed.

"But the corsets are too tight." I tried not to whine. I had the best of everything: clothes, food, and money. I also held the keys to freedom for hundreds of people.

"Rich people, royalty, they eat a lot. They're wasteful." Braden bemoaned to the ceiling and grimaced.

"But you had those things, right? I mean before?" I pried. He was always evasive about his growing up.

"Let's not talk about that now. This is about you." He kissed my forehead. "Do you feel alright?"

"I think I need the bathroom." I mumbled, but I didn't want to move. I had been anxious about the prior moments since we got married.

"Yep, you should." He sat up and moved the covers off. "Go on." He prodded.

I waddled into the bathroom. It burned when I urinated. When I wiped, there were just spots of watery blood. Not as bad as the stories I'd heard. I'd been pretending to be a good wife for four years now. It took that long to get brave enough to ask Braden for this night. I was over seventeen. I needed to start acting like an adult and that included sex. I could learn a lot from books and our good doctor, who was also part of the Underground. However, nothing could come close to the real experience.

I had to give Braden credit. He had to pretend the whole time too. Laughing with the other high ranked soldiers and officials about how many women in addition to their wives they had access to. He told me this not long after he revealed how they got Cissy out.

It was the day he and Micah had tested me, a few days after the draw. "You mustn't tell anyone, Lavinia. As I've said before, you know the risks. Any of us could die. Are you prepared to hear the truth?" The fourteen-year-old me wasn't ready, but I needed to know what happened to Cissy.

"Cissy was in danger Lavinia. The Lieutenant had been killing only white women. He would disappear for a while. I wasn't the only one that noticed." He sipped his tea. "I will tell you this in a blunt fashion, and I want you to understand, that it's not that I don't care. But these are the facts. Cissy's master only wanted her every once in a while."

He set down his cup and leaned back in his chair. "She was given other men to entertain, including the Lieutenant. She couldn't protest or tell a soul. He, well, um, damaged women. Beat them, cut them. He beat Cissy so badly that she was in the infirmary for two days. She couldn't tell anyone, but Dr. Gideon knew what was happening and relayed her story to me. He guessed, and I agree, that because he couldn't have you, he was going to take out his viciousness on her."

I cringed. Cissy had suffered for me. I hadn't even known.

"The night before the Draw was supposed to be the perfect opportunity to get her to freedom. Everyone would be distracted. The Colonel was dying. Soldiers were betting on picks. Servants and slaves were focused on what changes might happen with new mistresses or wives coming on. I knew that Cissy's master was tired of her not being around enough. Sure enough, he'd picked another mistress to be with. All I had to do was distract the Lieutenant. And I knew he wanted you." He paused.

I had been the bait. The room spun as sickness overwhelmed me.

"Breathe Lavinia." My Captain stood next to me and massaged my shoulder. "You helped save Cissy. I hadn't counted on him having killed all those young women. I thought a few maybe. I hoped the others had escaped. I'm certain that he would have killed her too, eventually. He was a very cruel man. He went to the cave that night to continue to abuse the dead bodies. Ultimately, he hung for his crimes. I had to wait for him to leave. Then wait again until very late in the evening to pretend that I had an impure interest in Cissy. I didn't need to worry, with all the activity, she was alone. I got her to an escape connection right before the sun rose. I had to go to the new Colonel with a select group of soldiers and showed him the cave. The Lieutenant left his personal marked items behind. It sealed his fate. I barely made it back in time for the Draw." His fingers released from my shoulder, and he sat back down.

"You must never tell anyone Lavinia. On top of that I'll

need your help. We can stop the people that do this. That continually harm people. You haven't had much say in your life so far. I can give you a choice."

I couldn't believe my ears. "What do you mean?"

"I can get you to freedom. You'll have to wait a while. And there's always a chance I'll get reassigned. I can't tell you exactly where or how or even if you have the slightest chance of rejoining your parents. But the opportunity is there." He refreshed our teas.

The Captain that had scared me on that first day we met in the fields could now give me freedom.

"Or, um, what else?" I was afraid to ask.

"You stay with me and help the Underground. You are intelligent, clever, kind, and charming. With more education, you'll be miles ahead of most women in the country. You'd be able to glean information from other high-ranking Redcoat and officials' wives. It will help me get others to freedom. You know you did this before, right?"

I shook my head.

"Lavinia, your parents were well linked to the Underground. You were their best spy."

I closed my eyes and I remembered Mama telling me not to be late for dinner. I was abandoned. Tears created long trickles down my blouse.

The Captain put his arm around me. "Don't be sad Lavinia. You helped people. If you stay, I can't promise that the work won't be hard. But you'll help others like your parents did."

"I-I don't know." I had no idea what I wanted.

"You are talented, Lavinia." Braden wooed me. "The older Redcoats still remember you as a child. I've heard them talk about you as if you were their grandchild. The younger ones, well, quite frankly, want you. If you had made it to the Draw on your sixteenth birthday, I'm certain that someone like the Sergeant would've picked you. That is if an official or another higher ranked officer like myself hadn't decided to pull you into the housemaids group first."

"You would've done that?"

"I could lie to you Lavinia, but I was already planning to. You didn't belong out there in the fields. You're pretty now, even crying your eyes out. In two years, you'll be stunning. I knew you were going to be a prized possession."

My body stilled. I didn't have choices before. "What do you want for me to do?"

"I'd like for you to stay. Know this, I can't protect you once you've gone. If you stay, I will do my absolute best to keep you safe."

I was in such a peculiar state. Days ago, I was destined to farm, then possibly marry a Redcoat. How could I possibly make such a decision? "Can I think about it?" I whispered.

"Yes. Until tomorrow. But promise me, don't try to escape on your own in the meantime. I don't want you to get hurt." He kissed my forehead and called for Micah. "Lavinia, you can trust Micah and Dr. Gideon for anything if I am gone, alright?"

"Yes, Sir."

"If you stay, remember to call me Braden at home, Captain in front of other military. Understood?"

"Yes Sir, I mean, Braden." I stuttered.

"Come, let's get more food in you. Whatever choice you make, well, it will take stamina."

That evening was without drama. After dinner, Braden left to tend to business with the new Colonel. I changed into one of the nicest nightdresses and robes I'd ever worn. I vacated my bedroom and tried to read in the library, but my mind wouldn't let me relax.

"Miss Lavinia, would you like a snack?" Micah came in with tea and more biscuits.

"Thank you, Micah."

He started to leave, and I called him back. "Can I ask you a question, Micah? Would you join me?"

"You're not used to being alone, are you?" He smiled.

"No." Micah already knew me well. "There's always been someone. Always chores, always work."

"You will have time for peace with the Captain. He is an honorable man."

"He helped you?" I raised a brow.

"Yes. And others. More than I can count. I was grateful. I decided to stay and help."

"Oh." I nibbled on the food.

"He won't say it aloud, and I don't want to make you feel guilty, but the Captain needs you, Miss Lavinia. Still, he wants you to have a choice."

"I know, thank you."

"You're a tough one. I couldn't believe you didn't crumble this afternoon." Micah ate with me. It was relaxing to have such calm company. "You'll make the right decision." He patted my hand and stood to leave. "Let me know when you're ready to turn in."

"I'll be ready soon." I agreed even though I still didn't quite know what to do.

It had been such a long day that I fell asleep right after Micah turned down the bed. Soon the Captain was there with me. He undressed in the darkness and slid beside me. His fingers felt good on my face. They moved down, flicked around my collar bone, and untied my gown. I sat up and he undressed me. The wetness of his kisses made me warm. They fluttered over my body. I ached with a desire I'd never had before. A loud bang awoke me from my dream.

There was a thunderstorm outside, and rain splattered the windows. Their shutters rattled in the wind.

The Captain strode in. "Lavinia? I thought I heard you stirring?"

"Yes. The storm scared me." I blushed.

The Captain came to my bedside. "Do you want me to stay?"

"Yes, please."

"Alright Lavinia, I'll be back in a moment."

I fidgeted nervously until he came back. He wasn't two steps in the door before I blurted out. "I want to stay."

"I'm glad you do." He grinned and climbed in next to me like he had before. It was good to feel safe again.

The next three years were a whole new experience. Micah schooled me in etiquette. My Captain taught me to use weapons deep in the forest. They both showed me where the long-rumored caves were and how to find them by knitted strings tied on certain trees in the forest. I learned everything and anything about the Underground.

It had commenced during the Civil War. When the Queen retook the Americas, the Underground continued to take anyone to freedom. There was another rumored group that helped to fund the rescues, but my Captain wasn't sure if it had a name. We didn't even know where freedom was. We just knew that no one ever came back.

"There is no rhyme or reason to when we get people out." Braden explained. "Resources can become available at any time. We don't want to set a pattern that someone could catch on to."

I helped others to freedom. Most days I went to tea with other officer wives to listen to every nugget from them. "You'll hear things you don't like, Lavinia. About other wives, mistresses, slaves. New ones, old ones. If it sounds like anyone is leaving or coming, even if you think it's just gossip, I need to know it all." Braden coached me.

I had to pretend that I was wiser beyond my years but strike a balance that implied that my husband was a gentleman and not a child molester. Most of the other brides were still in adolescence as well.

I read more books than I imagined existed. I didn't realize

that there were other languages in the world. I learned them from Micah.

Every once in a long while, the Captain and I were truly alone. Waiting in the forest for hours for an Underground contact to come to us. Sometimes exploring a new cave to see if it was suitable for hiding. I treasured these moments, for Braden let his guard down. He would delight in teaching me things. I would steal looks at him while my heart beat in happiness. I thanked God every day that he'd rescued me.

Our first kiss was during our brief wedding ceremony, a week after I decided to join the Underground. It was quick and sweet. They remained that way for a while.

We had to keep up appearances, but under the surface, we knew we could be discovered, our lives changed in an instant. We played the officer and his wife with just the right amount of public affection.

Tonight had changed everything. During a particular harrowing escape, we had to trudge through one of the small streams that lead to the river while in almost complete darkness. "Move slowly, don't slosh through the water." Braden ordered.

We each held onto a young girl. They were sisters brought into work. They had a free family to the far north. One of Braden's contacts made arrangements to pick them up in one of the caves.

But we hadn't planned on the new Colonel's dog. It got loose and was barking through the forest. "Turn off your lanterns. Get into the stream, it'll cut off the scent." The Captain whispered as two young Redcoat soldiers ran after the errant pup. The tips of their lighted bayonets were getting closer.

"Lean in behind this log." Braden guided us. Soon the

water was up to our chins. We shivered but didn't move an inch. The girls were only in night dresses.

"There he is!" We heard a soldier lunge. "Got him."

"Stupid dog. Colonel too damn lazy to get him himself." The other grumbled as they stumbled away. We waited until they had cleared the forest line.

"Whew that was close. Alright, I'll help you out." Braden jumped out of the water and onto the log. Then one by one he pushed us up and over to the bank. With a hiss of a lighter, he relit our lanterns. "This way." We walked for about fifteen minutes in the chilly autumn night before reaching the cave. An older black woman awaited us.

"Harriet? Mercy one." Braden whispered.

"Yes Captain. Mercy two." Even in the low light I could see her infectious grin "My, oh my, looks like you all went on a midnight swim."

"Someone had a dog." Braden laughed.

"Well, I'm gonna apologize, I had to travel light tonight, no coat, one lamp, and a satchel. Anything else would draw suspicion."

Braden hadn't put on a thick coat. I only wore a plain old dress. The girls were freezing, and you could see through their gowns.

Braden and I undressed. "Here take the coat, and the shirt." He handed the pieces off to the older girl.

I eased out of my dress and slid it over the younger one. "It's a little long on you, but at least you're covered. Good luck." I kissed them both on the cheeks.

Harriet laughed. "Well, that's one way to do it. Be blessed and safe now."

"You too Harriet." Braden said our goodbyes.

"We gotta get back. I can smell rain." He warned. We scattered off through the woods to the house. We stood at the tree line until we were certain no one was nearby. Micah signaled to us from his bedroom with another lantern. As we ran inside and headed straight for the warm kitchen, a storm broke out.

Micah joined us. "I have hot tea ready and—" He paused, giggled at me, and then went back to setting the tea. Braden did the same but didn't look away. I couldn't stop staring at him either.

He was bare chested with his wet suspenders clinging to his skin. The dark cloth of his trousers gathered around his crotch. My mouth fell open at the sight of his well-chiseled body.

"Lavinia, go upstairs and get warm, we'll bring your tea up shortly." He muttered.

"Oh." Despite the chill I was warm and tingly inside. I flew up the stairs to change. I grabbed my nightgown and stood before the mirror to see the damage to my undergarments. I instantly knew why my Captain had sent me upstairs. Only my waist cincher hid any part of my body. I could see completely through my pantaloons and undershirt. I'd never seen myself naked before. I remember seeing other women of all kinds without clothes. The most popular ladies had an hourglass figure, and right at this moment, so did I. I peeled away the layers and stole one last look. I wasn't vain in any sense, but what my Captain had told me before had come to fruition. I was beautiful.

I slipped on my gown and robe as I heard them approach up

the stairs. The knock on the door made me strangely nervous. "Here you are Mrs. Lavinia." Micah strolled in with the tray. "The Captain will be here in a moment."

"Thank you, Micah." I sat on the bed and tried to steady my hand to pour. Braden's body flashed through my mind. I inhaled deep breaths and finally was able to have tea. It seemed like an eternity before Braden knocked.

"May I come in?" Braden's eyes sparkled.

"Yes." I blushed.

"Lavinia, I want you to know that I care for you very much. But starting tonight, I can no longer sleep in your bed, well, without wanting to be with you. In the Biblical sense."

"I-I know." I flustered.

"You come to me when you are ready. But please, don't make it too much longer."

"Okay." I agreed. Braden began to leave. "No, I meant now."

"You're ready now?" He shut the door and came back towards the bed.

"Yes."

And so, I cleaned up after our first lovemaking. I hoped I wouldn't cry during the next time.

"Lavinia?" Braden called.

"Yes, I'm coming." I opened the bathroom door.

"Everything alright? Ready for bed, darling?" He cooed.

"Yes."

"Come stand by the bed."

I sheepishly crossed the room. I couldn't speak.

"Lavinia, I love you." He touched me again, feeling every inch of me. "Come get warm."

"I love you too." It was a blissful release to say it. I wondered if I had been dreaming everything. I fully expected to wake up in the dormitories the next morning.

I was enveloped in Braden's arms and near asleep when he whispered to me. "Tomorrow, I want to tell you everything. I need you to know. Understood?"

"Hmm. Yes."

7 A WORD ABOUT THE CAPTAIN

Fortunately for us, it continued to rain the whole next day. I was able to sleep in. I only woke when Braden left to make certain that nothing had changed in the Kingdom that would affect us. He kissed me with a promise that he'd be back. I easily fell back into slumber.

I woke again after ten. By the time I freshened up in the bathroom, Micah strolled in with breakfast.

"Good morning Mrs. Lavinia. How are you feeling this morning?" He had a full smile that showed every inch of his teeth. I was certain that he knew what happened last night.

"Very well, Micah, thank you." I mimicked his grin.

"The Captain wanted me to make sure that I checked in on you. To let you know that you could rest as long as you wanted and that if you needed Dr. Gideon, I could arrange for him to come to the house."

"I'm good."

"Very well then." He rose to leave.

"Did the Captain say when he'd be back?"

"After noon. I believe that he has lunch with the Colonel today. I know that he will want to spend time with you for the rest of the day." Micah paused in the doorway. "I'm glad to see you well."

"Thank you, Micah." I ate in a hurry and picked out a nicer dress. I couldn't wait for Braden to come home and tell me everything he wanted for me to know.

In our years together, I'd never seen my Captain like this. Absolutely broken and upset, his face in a mash of anguish as he paced in the library.

"Micah, please come in, shut the door behind you, and pour the good stuff."

Micah paled. He and I both knew that the Captain usually only drank alcohol to celebrate special occasions. But he didn't look happy.

In fact, when he walked in, he didn't even greet anyone. I could hear him the minute he walked in. Without hesitation he ordered Micah, "Be wary. Be absolutely on point with anyone who comes to the door. Where's Lavinia?"

"In the library, Sir."

"Good. I want you to go upstairs and look outside. Get a visual on anything that might be wrong or out of place. Then report to me in the library."

When Micah joined us and finally poured the drinks, we were on the edge of our seats in suspense. "First, in case we are interrupted, I want you to be ready. Act as if nothing is wrong. We were all home last night. Understood?"

As Micah and I both agreed. My stomach clinched.

"Very good. I will say this as succinctly as possible. The two girls we sent out for freedom last night didn't make it. Harriet put them on a train to the North. The train was stopped in Chicago this morning, they were discovered, and questioned. The girls said that they were from here. However, according to the Redcoat that informed the Colonel, they were very confused. They thought 'here' was further south, Mississippi, not Missouri. They remembered the Colonel, the Sergeant, and me by our looks." Braden drank more of the brandy Micah had poured. "But the girls suddenly died in custody, during questioning. The authorities wired the Colonel to see if anyone was missing. Sure enough, they'd been gone after bed check in the dorm last night."

"What, what happened? How'd they die?" I couldn't believe my ears. Micah gazed out the window with a sad look on his face.

"Lavinia, the girls were poisoned." Tears welled up in Braden's eyes. "They didn't know."

"What? What didn't they know?" I was more scared than I'd ever been.

"Harriet gave them vials filled with perfumed oil. Or at least that's what the girls thought. Harriet told them that, if they should be caught, to drink it. The oil would make them feel better." Braden sipped from his brandy again. "When the conductor found them, they got scared and they, well, they drank the oil."

"I—I don't understand."

"Mrs. Lavinia, honey." Micah whispered. "The oil was from hemlock. The girls were too young to know any better. The Redcoats would've beaten them to death to get answers out of them. It was better this way, dear, they didn't suffer."

"Oh, oh dear God." I shuddered and mourned with Micah and my Captain. "Are we monsters?"

"No Lavinia. It's crucial to the Underground to keep all of our secrets. Again, they would've tortured them. Even if they gave them the right answers, told them everything they knew, they still would've hurt or killed them."

"Mercy. Lavinia, those girls died so we could live." Micah touched my hand. "You should cry for them."

Braden stood and wiped his eyes. "I was to have lunch with the Colonel to discuss other things. The telegram arrived right as we began to eat. Fortunately for us, the girls died before they could give out any other information. The Colonel prodded me. Of course, I pretended that I was home all evening, and Micah would certainly attest to that. The Colonel was with his mistress, the Sergeant with his wife. We went and questioned their bunkmates. None of them knew anything. But we need to be vigilant. It's drawn unwanted attention to the village from higher ups in the Kingdom. We may need to find other ways to help, but for now, we need to lay low, we can't offer assistance."

I whimpered.

"Micah, if you would leave now, please. I need to discuss other business with my wife."

"Yes, Sir." As he exited, Braden sat next to me.

"Lavinia, I know that this is frightening. But I've seen worse, I want you to understand."

"How can it be any worse?" I sobbed. I couldn't believe the two scared children that I aided the night before were dead.

"Those girls could've been given to some of the worst men

in the Kingdom. Hell, on the planet. Men like the Lieutenant."

"You know this for sure?"

"Yes, because it happened to me." Braden's face was pale, and I could see absolute destruction in his eyes.

Braden told me of his haunted past. "In England, when I was young, my family was starving. My father had been injured in the Royal Navy. His leg was crushed during a kind of unauthorized activity. He got pinned between two ships. I think that it was because he was helping less fortunate people. He may have been helping others escape. Nevertheless, they had to cut it off at the knee. He was handicapped with a peg leg. They said he wasn't needed anymore, that he was dismissed. My father was a good man, Lavinia. He did everything he could to help. I think his commander didn't like it and forced my father out.

Mother had been married before, divorced with two children. My father loved her and my stepsisters. Then I came along." Braden moved my hair aside to gauge my reaction.

"My mother had been spoiled. Her first husband had money. But he abandoned her and her girls. She hounded my father, and she drank whatever money we had. She tore him apart emotionally. She became the mistress of one of his best friends that was still in the Navy."

"My father eventually went to find work. He never came back. Or I may never know if he did, because two days after he'd gone, we were out of money. We were forced out of our home. We moved to a boarding house. When we couldn't pay the rent, we were forced out of there too. My sisters refused to work. After a year of moving from place to place with no hope in sight, they ran away.

"The new Kingdom order was brutally enforced. We were lower class. My mother was still pretty, and she became a mistress to a soldier. But she wanted more. And she couldn't get enough spirits. She stole from the soldiers' pantry. She whored herself out. I watched her spiral into a decrepit hag."

I could barely believe what I was hearing. My Captain, who was eloquent and polished, was as poor a soul as I. "I'm so, so sorry."

"Don't be. I was luckier than most. The last soldier my mother was with, was evil. He threatened to cut her off unless he could have me."

My eyes narrowed in confusion.

"He was what they call a pedophile, Lavinia. He liked young boys. He repeatedly raped me. In return, he rewarded my mother with alcohol."

I dropped my glass. "No, oh no."

Braden swiped the errant glass from the floor and set it on the table with a dull thud. "Again, I was better off, because one night, when the soldier was done with me, he and my mother were too inebriated to watch me. I was about seven years of age. I went out into the street to look for food. A Vicar walking his dog saw me. He and his wife couldn't have children of their own and they took me in. They would tell me later, that I was so frightened that I didn't speak for weeks. And that was only after they continually tempted me with sweets. My shyness was a godsend, for I focused on learning. I became intelligent beyond my years."

"The ministers above the Vicar attended to royalty. They were well off. I was given a good education, food, and clothing. I was given their names. As I grew old enough to understand what had happened to me, I began to notice things."

"My new parents would take extra food or clothing out on certain evenings. The Vicar would attend to sick folk of the parish or something of that nature. Or that's what I was told."

"By the time I reached my teens, they explained that there were literally thousands of others out there like me. People that needed help. There were covert groups around the world, like here, like the Underground, that were helping people bound in captivity, slaves to the soldiers. I agreed to help them."

"I was less awkward than most young men. I had more schooling, knowledge. My parents had contacts on both sides of the Kingdom. I was recruited into the military and fast tracked to be an officer. They sent me to help industrialize the Kingdom. First, just outside of London, then to Manchester, Birmingham, and further on to other parts of Europe. I was trusted so much that they sent me here because of how good the soil produced food. For my work with the Underground, here was a network rich with possibilities for rebellion."

"Each place I was sent to had contacts to those freedom groups. I continued to free and recruit others. When I came here Lavinia, I'd already been given much higher duties. I successfully completed missions while masquerading as a Redcoat Captain."

"That is until last night. Last night was my first complete failure. I am still worried that we might be eventually questioned. However, the lunch with Colonel today was going to be about my increased duties. He wants to send me to Virginia for several months."

"You're leaving? When?" I had just started to feel safe. The rollercoaster of emotions was making me mad.

"Soon, but you'll be coming with me."

I sighed with relief. "I'm grateful."

"I am grateful too Lavinia, that I rescued you, one of my best saves, an incredible stroke of luck. You were a pretty girl on the verge of womanhood. I honestly don't know how you managed to survive, other than with the help of Cissy and Ida. When I saw you in the field that day, and then heard how intelligent you were, I could see that my time was limited before another soldier would take you. I had hoped to have you work here with Micah before the Draw, but new equipment had arrived. And the Lieutenant's sour reputation with the Underground made it impossible to focus on much else.

My mouth was agape. "You came for me?"

"Yes, you were one reason. I needed to recruit a female because the Underground and the other freedom groups are going to try and take down the Kingdom from the inside."

8 PASSAGES

Virginia

"Now, you can't be afraid of nothin' Missus. You walk all quiet like. Just like a cat. A shadow in the night. Can't be seen or heard. Now come this way." Earl's thick southern accent encouraged me. The elderly former slave survived the takeover by remaining with the Underground Railroad. It was referred to as the Underground now, for everyone was a slave to the Monarchy.

We were in an abandoned farmhouse in Virginia. The only light came from a lazy late autumn full moon. It was one of my last eves in that state before Braden was ordered back to Missouri. We were only supposed to visit a while to implement new equipment into the coal mines. We ended up staying for over five years. There were short visits back to Missouri to update the Colonel on advances in machinery and the like. Micah kept our Underground line open there as best as he could with little support. The Colonel apparently needed Braden's expertise for more than just quick consultations. For once our work was done in Virginia, we were to return. That day was rapidly approaching.

I slid around the perimeter of the room so stealth fully that the only sound you could hear was the ticking of Earl's pocket watch. It was an uncomfortable reminder that time was running out. The Kingdom continued to build unlimited resources.

I ignored the sweat that rolled down the back of my neck

and continued. I left and then came back inside without a peep. I lifted my chin and exhaled. Braden nodded with approval.

"Well done, Missy. Whelp, I'm on my way." As Earl strained for his cane, the Captain jumped forward to assist him out. My face flushed with recognition of Braden's strength and kindness. He was the only man I'd ever known other than my father. But I had to pretend that I knew men and very, very well. My Captain would train me in those ways too.

Our time in Virginia had been more than productive for the Kingdom. Braden had begun training me to fight, to steal, and to spy. He put me in even better hands with Earl. Earl, like Harriet, had worked with the Underground in every aspect: from housing, to procuring meals for the less fortunate, and the hardest challenge of all, getting escapees to freedom. Earl was getting on in years. He couldn't move very well, and his facilities were starting to fail. But he could still train others to do as he had.

My time in the fields made me strong enough to handle hard tasks without much sleep, water, and food. I had one last test before returning to Missouri.

There were times that the coal mines in Virginia made the fields in Missouri look like a tea party. Slaves went deep underground for at least twelve hours at a time. They were poorly equipped for such a hideous job. Tools weren't strong enough for the layers of hard black earth. The workers came to the surface covered in dirt, cuts, and bruises. Most died after only less than a year of inhaling toxic soot and fumes, all for the Queen.

Braden had worked hard with a group of inventors to create digging machines, picks made from the strongest wood and steel. Their best invention was an amphibious mask that would filter out the poisons and allow workers to breathe clean air. If put at a

A Long Reign

proper setting, it could be used underwater.

The local officials finally agreed to changes after seeing that the high turnover in slaves was costing them money. The only problem was that they wanted to wait another year before implementing the new equipment. I remember Braden's frustration.

"These people are dying Lavinia, hundreds a year. They could have much more coal, more power. Yet they'd rather have people die for less." Braden unbuttoned his shirt and threw it aside in frustration as I waited for him to come to bed. "Another two men died today. One of the wives died yesterday." He yanked off his boots and socks with the same passion.

"What can we do about it?" At this point in our marriage, I knew that to get him thinking proactively would help tame his anger.

"I'm thinking of smuggling in the equipment. At the very least the masks." He undid his bracers and let his trousers drop. He was handsome while near naked and angry. I struggled to suppress a giggle. "What's funny?" He pouted.

"You're just, um, passionate. I guess."

"I am, about you too." He jumped into the bed and covered my face with tender kisses. He stopped. "Did you have a good study with Earl today?"

"Braden!"

"I need to ask, Lavinia. Remember, I didn't just marry you for your good looks." He got a dig in. "I mean, that was a part of it."

"It was good. He reminded me how to watch people. We

went to town to buy items for our return home. At every opportunity, he pointed out things I should notice, like where carriages park and who's in them. Is anyone dressed differently, as if they're new in town? I easily picked out two new Redcoat recruits that arrived."

"Well done, Madam." My Captain complimented while pulling off my gown. "And you know, you've expanded your repertoire. You are talented in other areas."

I closed my eyes as his lips met mine again. He sent tremors through me with the grace of his fingertips. For the next moments he was mine. I didn't want to share him with anyone else, soldiers, slaves, or the Kingdom. I would collapse easily beneath him.

We lay in complete bliss afterwards. Braden stared out the window at a starry sky.

"We're going to do a lot more than just smuggle in masks, aren't we?"

"Yes, yes we are."

I tried not to panic as the steamboat Horizon lurched sideways. I leisurely strolled past Redcoats who sprang into action on the sinking steamer. This was definitely not part of Braden's plan to get fifty slaves freed before we returned to Missouri.

The Kingdom had given in to a request to try the ventilation masks for the mines. But there was a provision that they be tried on fifty slaves that were brought in from further south and by steamship so that the trains carrying coal wouldn't be disrupted.

Braden had volunteered to escort the slaves and precious

cargo.

Earlier on this cool autumn eve, we met the ship upriver. The slaves were "troubled creatures" according to their former masters. More than half were linked to the Underground and had paid for their silence during questioning with burns, whip marks, and scars from all kinds of brutal torture. They were of all races, male and female.

As we boarded, Braden confirmed that he knew at least six of the workers. Slaves he'd either helped free or ones that helped others escape. He hoped to give all of them a second chance.

The plan was to get keys for their shackles before we even departed the dock. That would be handled by a purser on the steamer who was very familiar with the workings of the Underground. There was a stop mid-point in a farming village. The ever-greedy Kingdom wanted to save more money; thus, the Horizon was going to take on another load. Hundreds of sacks of grain were added to the ship, while only delivering about twenty-five crates to a group of farmers. Those crates would be filled with escaping human cargo thanks to our helpful purser.

The send-off went as planned. Most of the Redcoats were preoccupied with whores and gambling aboard the boat. Braden made sure that copious amounts of food and alcohol were available to all the troops.

"Is this your lovely wife?" The Horizon's first mate drawled as I helped serve a more refreshments to a thirsty group of high ranked officers.

"Yes, this is Lavinia." Braden charmed. I think he didn't have to fake much on this trip. I wore an outrageously low-cut gown with a long bunch slit up the side.

"Hmmm, very nice." The mate almost drooled on me. I pretended to like the attention while I poured his liquor. I soon exited to check on the progress of our shipment.

As I approached the lower deck, the purser popped out. "Mrs. Lavinia, we have a problem. Two Redcoats were sent in to watch the slaves. They're unshackled but are pretending to be bound. We couldn't get them into the boxes. What should I do?"

My heart sank. "I'll get with the Captain. Maybe we can say the crates were refused at mid-point? Then we'll get them delivered in town. They'll have to wait on the dock. We'll just get these two Reds distracted soon."

"Yes Ma'am." He hurried off while I bolted back to the ballroom.

"Did you miss me, darling?" I slid into Braden's lap. He instantly knew something was wrong.

"Of course, I'll always want you. Excuse me gentlemen, I have business to attend to." Braden carried me out to the sounds of guffaws from the others.

We didn't go to our cabin. We bolted outside where no one wanted to be in the chilly air. "What happened?"

"Two guards were brought down. The purser can't get them into the crates in time for mid-point."

"And what did you say?"

"That perhaps the crates would get refused. And then we'd take them all the way down? We'd get time to distract them on the second half of the trip. It was the only palpable solution."

"Alright. Good thinking, Lavinia. We should be getting to

mid-point in about fifteen minutes. We'll take on the grain and keep the crates. I'll let our contact know to wait outside of town at the finish. We'll free the slaves two to three hours after we dock. I'll send another soldier in at mid-point to say he needs the other Redcoats for delivery. The pursuer should be able to handle them then but be ready to help."

"Yes Sir, Captain." I grinned wickedly.

"Hmm, you'd better save those dirty thoughts for later. Now mess up my hair like you just did what you were thinking." Braden drew me close and kissed me with such passion that I thought we might actually have just enough time to enjoin in some holy matrimony. He stopped. "No more distractions. Be safe."

We waltzed back to our respective posts. I waited outside the ballroom until Braden was settled. My Captain sat down for another round. The mate burst into laughter at his appearance.

"Well now, that's some wife you got there."

"Yes, she's quite the lady." The minute they drew hands, I was off to see the purser.

The docking was gratefully uneventful. The slaves pretended to be restless but remained falsely enchained. The two Redcoat guards were pulled to help with the loading of the hundreds of sacks into the upper cargo hold. They were swayed to assist with a reward of female entertainment for their services. The purser and I escorted two slaves into each crate.

The upper ranks were drunk enough that Braden and I were certain our alternative plan would work. They didn't even stop gambling while the boat received new cargo. I poured yet another round as we embarked on part two of our journey. "You gentlemen enjoy all this. There's plenty here." I cooed. "I'll just need to get a bit more." I set my serving tray down, slipped a last bottle of liquor down my blouse, strolled back into the hot kitchen, and headed for the cargo hold.

We weren't two minutes from the dock when the Horizon began to list. None of us had counted on it being overloaded. The large steamer tilted horribly to the left, throwing its passengers aside. The ship groaned as the steam engine strained to push the massive weight forward to no avail.

The snapping of ornamental wooden posts could be heard. Screams and hollers echoed through the hallways. I feigned calmness as I passed soldiers running to and fro. "Abandon ship! Abandon ship!"

It took forever to get to the cargo hold. I was shocked to see the gate was locked and the frightened face of the purser behind it.

"What happened?"

"A soldier I hadn't seen before locked us in just a moment ago. He didn't see me. I was checking on all the slaves and bent over a crate when I heard the gate slam and lock. What the hell is going on?"

"The ship is sinking." And as if on cue, water started to come into the hallway I stood in. "No key?" I sputtered as the river brushed against my toes. I had to get to Braden for help.

"No." We pulled on the iron gate in vain.

"Gun, axe, crowbar? Anything?"

"Just a hammer and crowbar. That's not going to move this."

"What did the Redcoat look like?"

"I didn't see him. But I think he was smoking a pipe. The tobacco was different. Um, I think it was a foreign plant of sorts." Water was filling to my ankles and poured down to the steps into the hold.

"Alright, remove the slaves from the crates. And get out the respiratory masks. Everyone gets one. All they have to do is press the green button. The tank that's attached should fill them with air. Do it now." I could hear them pounding and helplessness washed over me. "I'll be back, I promise." I held a deep breath and tried to smell a different kind of tobacco, whatever that might be.

I went up and out to the nearest deck and thanked God above, for there at the rail was a Redcoat smoking an odd pipe with a set of keys dangling from his hip. The ship reared again, and I slid right into him. He reeked of liquor and something else I couldn't place. He was oblivious that the steamer was going down.

"Well, hellooo, Missy."

"Hello, darling. Enjoying the moonlight?" I tried to remain calm. Time was fleeting. Water was flowing up to where we stood, which meant the cargo holds were almost under.

"Yeah, and you. I think I could enjoy you." He laughed to the sky. "Howl at the moon!" As he hollered, I yanked the bottle from my cleavage and hit him square on the back of his head. Glass joined the river that ran over the bottom rung of the ship rail. I snatched the keys from his hip.

"Uh why'd you do that for?" He muttered and fell into the river. I tried to ignore my guilt at killing a man and sloshed over to the steps.

I hated being right. Water was climbing up the stairs. The hold was under it. I'd have to swim down. I exhaled and dove in.

Just as I approached the locked gate, the ship's lights went out. The purser and the faces of the slaves were lit in the strange green glow of the masks. He touched my hand and guided me to the lock. After two tries, I got it. He pushed it open as I reached back for the stairs and headed up with all of them behind me.

It was dark and I was disoriented. I could barely grasp the rail which was completely immersed. Just as I was losing breath, a set of strong arms gathered around me.

The cool air of the night snapped me awake as I gasped. "Lavinia!" Braden had searched what he could of the ship before securing a rowboat by the hold. I panted as he gathered me in. I saw Braden gesturing wildly above me as I finally got enough oxygen. "Are you alright?" He wrapped me in a woolen blanket and helped me upright.

"Yes, yes. I think."

"Look!" We peered out to the river's edge as a line of low green lights emerged on the shoreline far from where the Redcoats had abandoned ship and deserted their human cargo to die. "They're free. Lavinia, you did it." His face was illuminated in blue from the moonlight. He pecked me on the cheek, grabbed the oars and rowed us to shore. By the time we reached sand, the Horizon gushed and bubbled to the bottom of the river.

"Lavinia, I know you're tired, but we have to join the Redcoats. We'll have to let them think that the workers and the purser drowned. But I'll be happy to carry you if you'd like."

"Yes please." I was weary. Even standing didn't feel right. Soon I was scooped up in his familiar embrace with the sounds of leaves crunching underfoot.

"I killed a man." My body ached and I could barely talk.

"But you saved fifty." Braden soothed as he helped me undress. Layers of thick fashionable clothing enveloped me. I procured new clothing the minute we joined the Redcoats at the dock. I stole it from another woman's trunk that had been spared. An officer's wife shouldn't look like a slut on dry land, I mused.

It was well after midnight by the time we reached our cabin that had been our home for the last several years.

Braden had been remarkably cleared from all responsibility for the Horizon's plunder. The ship's captain had lied about the steamer's capacity, size, and age. Under pressure from officials, he caved in questioning and even revealed that the hull was starting to rot from the inside. He was hung that night, even before we left the village.

"You did what was right, Lavinia." He slipped a warm nightdress over me as I sat shivering on the bed. "Let me stoke the fire." His wet clothes were still plastered to his body as he poked at the logs. "Better?"

"Hmm, yes." I poured tea at bedside. Our servants had already been reassigned to other soldiers. Doubt lingered in my mind about how I slugged the soldier into the murky depths.

My Captain finally undressed, the soaked clothing plopping to the floor in an ungodly mess. "That can be dealt with tomorrow." He strolled to the bed completely unashamed of his natural state. I warmed and it was more than just the tea.

"It's troubling you, isn't it?" He tossed the covers aside and climbed in next to me.

I couldn't hold it in. The tears escaped my eyes. I sipped tea, then set down my cup, and reached for a napkin.

"Oh, Lavinia. For all that you have endured, you have such a good heart. We do things that seem wrong. Look at me darling." He held my chin in his hand. His eyes were wet as well. "I was afraid I wouldn't find you. You have made my life bearable. We—I have done things. Irreparable damage to others. Suffered losses that cannot be undone. If I had lost you, I don't know how I would've continued. But we must. Many are still suffering." He held me close as he put out the light. "There is so much work to be done Lavinia. Know that I love you and I have faith that we will prevail. But tonight, we rest." He was asleep in short order. I didn't seem to sleep until much later despite how tired I was.

The room was already tidied up by the time I rose. Braden strolled in while putting on his coat. "Good morning. Lavinia, my love." I leaned in to receive his kiss as he came to the bed.

"Umm, good morning."

"Do you think you could dress quickly? I have breakfast ready. We have an opening, just enough time to go see Earl before we go. I think he'd love to hear how you rescued people last night. I'll even help you dress." Braden winked.

"Yes!" I stretched and leapt from the bed. For once I didn't mind my Captain hurrying me along.

We scurried through the foggy mountain morning to Earl's safe house in the woods where he lived with his niece, Verna. Braden's assumption that the town was still entranced with the sinking of the Horizon was correct. Everyone went down to the dock to see what remained of the sunken ship in daylight.

As we approached, Verna cried over a fire pit outside the cabin. She instinctively grabbed a rifle when she heard us approach the campsite.

"Captain and Mrs. Lavinia!" She dropped the weapon and ran to us. "My Uncle Earl is dead."

9 A BITTER HARVEST

"Lavinia, we need to talk about the possibility that I may not make it." Braden gazed out the train window before looking back at me.

"Earl's death was a reminder, wasn't it?"

"Yes. Verna will carry on his duties. If any of us is discovered, others have to step up." While our previous days had been quite the adventure, today it was as if reality had crashed inside our bedroom and shook us from a dream. I didn't like when Braden acted very stern, practical. It was times like these that I recognized a distance between us. "I heard rumors amongst the ranks after the Horizon sank. There's been a lot of upheaval in the Kingdom. Officials have disappeared or been executed. They are pushing for progress at unheard of speeds. It's unfortunate that they didn't see how well the masks worked, even under water."

"What do you think is going to happen?"

He grimaced. "I have a lot of knowledge. It's been noticed. I'll be moved into more constricted higher positions, of that I'm certain. We will have to leave things and well, people behind. Hopefully to England. One day, you may have to do it without me." His deep brown eyes cut into me. I observed his love for me in those same eyes the night before. His capacity to change his emotions at a moment's notice was disturbing.

"I just want you to remember everything that Earl taught you. Everything you've learned. I want you to be ready, no matter where we are or what happens. Promise me."

"I promise."

"Good." He dug into our scones, but I wasn't very hungry.

Missouri

It should have been a glorious autumn day, even in the horrifying political climate we lived in. The dawn revealed a cloudless brilliant blue sky. A cool October wind blew over the tips of the corn stalks, rustled through their leaves, and caused the plump corn husks to bob against each other.

We picked up directly where we'd left off. Micah had updated our contacts and the Underground was able to move through the village again.

The Colonel had amassed wealth and prestige that drew the attention of those close to the Queen. He was happy to see Braden and his prized knowledge back into the fold in Missouri. We were now guests at the Colonel's mansion at least once a week much to the delight of the Colonel's new wife, Josephine.

Although Josephine was close to birthing their first child, I could feel her watching me from the moment I entered their home. "You must come visit more often. I'm certain that we have much we could share."

"I'd be delighted." I feigned. We now had another in for possible information. It could possibly cost me some dignity, but I had to prepare for anything.

Braden began to stay overnight at the mansion, five to six times a week. I tried not to worry about how much danger he was in. I shook away those thoughts to focus on the task in front of me.

I stood with my Captain at the top of the hill that overlooked one of the best corn fields in the country. It was a flat plain, nestled between rolling hills, and alongside a spring fed creek. The untainted water kept the soil moist even after a dry, hot summer. The fertile ground was well known to produce the sweetest corn in the country.

The Colonel had ordered a spectacular luncheon to be served to the Redcoat upper crust to celebrate the harvest. Dignitaries had even come from the world capitol. Lower ranks of soldiers stood around the edges of the corn rows as slaves toiled away. There would not be any escapees today.

The best of the female servants and soldiers' wives had been brought to the hilltop to prepare the meal. We tried to be inconspicuous as possible, but it was clear that some of us could be nighttime companions for our guests. I thanked God that I was espoused to Braden.

There was one man who stood apart from the rest. He was a thick and tall elderly man. He wore a dark black dining suit instead of a uniform, while his unruly mop of grey thinning hair danced in the wind. His coal black eyes glared at the women around him. One glance at him gave me shivers. I overheard the Colonel introduce him. "Gentlemen, please welcome our guest from the capitol, Dr. Carthage. Please be seated."

The Redcoats, including my Captain, gathered around the table as we fluttered about in preparation. I dared not look in his direction.

"Today, we introduce our new harvest machines. Ones that can do the jobs of twenty men." The Colonel boasted. "A toast to progress." Glasses were raised and a chorus of "here, here" echoed over the meal.

Drivers secured their goggles and climbed ladders to small cages atop the impressive metal machines. With a quick yell from a foreman, they roared to life, their steam blackening the sky with puffs of poisoned smoke. They had to be at least fifteen feet high and ten feet wide. It took only six of them to cover the far end of the field. Two sets of blades on the front of each machine moved. The first set clipped at the robust husks, while the second pair slashed them to bits. Buckets on their backsides caught their reaping. Their massive wheels bore through the soft earth, leaving deep grooves behind. Even at our height, about fifty feet above the row, I could see the confusion spreading amongst the more than sixty field workers.

My heart dropped. Ida was still assigned to field duty. I'd only had one brief contact with her since my return. She had grown into one of the best farmers. There was no doubt in my mind that she was among the rows of corn. I didn't have a clue how they were supposed to work next to the machines.

The blades clanged loudly below while the superiors at our table ate. As the machines pushed forward, the workers began to panic. At first, they just moved further down the row. But as slaves tried to exit the field, they were shot or stabbed by the lighted bayonets of the soldiers that lined the perimeter of the field. My head spun. There was no way I could help any of the people in the field.

Soldiers glanced up from their food as shots rang out. "Oh, don't worry men, they'll get them all." Dr. Carthage chuckled as he dug into his meal.

I heard horrific screams as workers were sucked into an agonizing death. You knew a human died when one of the machines stuttered and belched an extra puff of smoke.

I brought more food to the table, near my Captain. Braden pretended to wipe his mouth with his napkin but whispered discreetly to me. "Look away Lavinia. Focus on serving." He ordered me. My hands trembled as I continued to fill massive platters with mounds of steaming roasted chicken.

"We will separate the wheat from the chaff. Or in this case, the corn from the husk and the skin from the bone." Dr. Carthage spoke with a furled lip. "Faster and more efficiently than ever before."

I desperately tried to hold back the bile in my throat as the acrid smells of burnt and mutilated human remains arrived with the fall wind that blew up the hillside. Most of the officers put down their forks as the stench wafted about. In their zeal to show off their genocide, the Colonel and Dr. Carthage hadn't counted on an odor assault from the havoc below.

"Ah, there can never be progress without a little pain." Dr. Carthage chortled and then licked a chicken bone clean, clearly impervious to the vile smelling destruction.

"Girls, move this indoors, now!" The Colonel barked furiously. Even he was turning a grey green amongst the horrific gasses of carnage.

Everyone choked back vomit as I desperately grabbed as many platters of food as I could carry into the temporary mess tents. Other servers held their aprons over their mouths while tears streamed down their smoke-stained cheeks. I don't think I'd ever seen such a large table cleaned and moved so briskly.

We reset the table to perfection inside the canopy as officers swilled as much wine and beer as they could hold to drown down the taste of sickness from their bellies. None of the Redcoats chided the help for sneaking in sips alongside them. Tent side flaps were tied down and oil lamps lit to halt the incriminating smells of death.

As male servants rushed the last panel down, I shuddered as I noticed that Dr. Carthage remained in his seat outside, seeming to enjoy the thick smoke that encompassed him.

A touch on my shoulder snapped me to attention.

"Don't turn around. Meet me at the cave tonight. 10 p.m. Just be there, no matter what." Braden whispered. "Nod if you understand."

I dipped my chin and continued to collect more food for the table. It was a waste of time though. No one had any appetite.

I was grateful for the full harvest moon that night. I didn't dare bring a lamp with me to the cave. I could barely breathe after not being able to eat any lunch or dinner that day. I was temporarily separated from Braden. He had been ordered to stay at the Colonel's mansion during Dr. Carthage's visit.

I stood at the entrance of the cave and swallowed before giving code. "Mercy one."

"Mercy two." Braden's pleasant lilt echoed as he lit a lamp about fifteen feet away. I could hear bats screech and flutter in the deeper bowels of the cave.

I couldn't hold back. I ran to him and buried my face into his jacket. My sobs racked my body as he embraced me. "Let it out. Cry now for Ida and the others. You know you won't be able to later." His fingers sifted gently through my hair as I gushed the withheld agony. "Alright now. Compose yourself. Remember, this is for the better. We do this for the better."

"Yes, yes. For the better." I repeated and moved back.

"Come sit down. You must be famished." He'd put down a blanket and procured dried fruits and nuts from his satchel as we relaxed in the cool air of the cave.

I was exhausted. Even though the evening was spent just studying, my mind wouldn't rest. Braden spoke as if he could read my mind.

"You'll have to forget. Not entirely. I want you to have purpose for our fight. Don't let it stop you from our focus. This could take months, years. God knows how long. None of us knew what Dr. Carthage had planned today. However, I did find out what he might do next."

"Really?" I spoke between the crunches of nuts and seeds in my mouth.

"Carthage noticed of you." His face was grim.

I froze. The pit in my stomach grew. "No—"

"Don't panic. Don't stop eating, you need nourishment." He pulled a canteen from his bag. "Warm milk. Drink it."

I sipped and started. "I don't—"

"Eat and listen." Braden remained stern. "Of course, you stand out from the others. That's what I wanted, but not for him. That's for the future. He wanted to meet you, but we got lucky. The Colonel's new wife is at the very start of labor tonight. I gambled when I noticed she didn't show for the luncheon today. I remembered that she liked you. Maybe in a prurient way, but I reminded the Colonel. He agreed that you should be with her tomorrow. I was able to arrange this before Dr. Carthage requested you."

"Oh God." I had helped deliver children all the time in the village. These were women I knew. And they didn't want to sleep with me.

"All you have to do is help deliver that baby. Soothe his wife. Pamper Josephine and help the midwife. Do whatever it takes. It could be our ticket out, a promotion. We could be sent to England earlier than expected."

"Promise her a little recovery romance later?" I teased.

"Not unless I'm watching." He bantered back while pulling another satchel out. "Here, I have fresh clothes for you. And a gift, she likes material things, remember? A pearl pendant. It's in a silk bag at the bottom."

"And afterwards?"

"Hopefully that baby will take its sweet time coming. Carthage is supposed to head out tomorrow night. Something about the bodies being fresh…" Braden's voice stilled.

"That was gruesome." I choked. "Ida's gone."

"At least we weren't on the ground. The guards down there were splattered with blood and dirt. You couldn't tell what was what on their coats. These men were seasoned soldiers, yet each of them looked as if they'd seen their last."

"I can't imagine." Tears escaped from my eyes.

"Good, then don't. Get mentally prepared for tomorrow. I'll be out in the field for the next week. I've got everything you need to stay here overnight. As soon as daylight breaks, you need to be at the Colonel's."

"You have to go now?" I whispered.

"Not until you're done eating first."

"What if I wanted dessert first?" I flirted openly. We were never alone enough anymore.

"Oh, have I trained you well. Nice try on the stalling tactic."

"Well, a kiss then?" I pouted.

"Just a kiss? Really now, Mrs. Lavinia." He drew me to him. I had missed how he smelled. The strength of his arms around me. "You may have more than a kiss." And he did much more than just a kiss.

When Braden had gone, the moon was setting as the sun rose. Both celestial gifts of the heavens glowed amber orange. I checked and rechecked my supplies. I set out for the Colonel's home about two miles from the cave.

The Colonel's wife had been able to sleep most of the night and into the day. Josephine didn't even start serious contractions until late the next night. God blessed us all with a robust baby boy.

Josephine liked her gift so much so that she asked if I could help whenever available. After the birth, the Colonel was so grateful for my assistance that he wondered aloud if I would be able to join them for a return to England. A lofty official had been impressed with his bitter harvest. He and all the other officers beneath him were promoted, including my Captain. We were all reassigned to London.

10 THE MAKER

The things I later learned about Dr. Carthage would horrify even the hardest of souls.

When Braden and I arrived at our home after the departure of Dr. Carthage and Josephine's completed labor, Micah's appearance echoed ours. We were all disheveled, exhausted, and mentally beaten.

"I'd never seen anything like that. Ever. This is a madman. A true bastard." We sat at the dining table in night clothes even though it was after two in the afternoon. Braden stared into nothingness as he spoke. "Even the Colonel was disgusted."

"I'm sorry about Ida, Lavinia." Micah touched my shoulder, put tea and snacks down, and joined us at the table. "You have my deepest sympathies."

"Thank you, Micah." Anger rose up in me like a cobra unfurled. "No one should be reduced to body parts to be used for consumption."

A knock at the door interrupted our conversation. Micah rose to get the expected delivery. A non-descript slave arrived. He had a large basket of goods and supplies. Some had come via locomotive, some from the farm. A thin, hidden package at the bottom of the delivery had definitely come by train.

"Thank you, young man." Micah closed the door, set the

package down, and waited. Braden and I pretended to enjoy our tea with faux smiles and snatches of conversation. Precisely three minutes later, Micah entered the dining room, flipped on our pricey new electric lamps, and closed the curtains. "Retrieving the basket, Captain."

I rose and moved our food tray aside. We may not have an appetite after what we were to review.

Micah came back with the basket. With a whoosh, it was on the table and soon emptied of its contents. The prized package was wrapped in plain brown paper and sealed with a string of twine so as not to raise suspicion.

The other items were soon whisked away by Micah. Braden snipped at the twine with a pocketknife to reveal a thin booklet stuffed with as much information as could be hidden in it.

I moved in closer to my Captain as Micah rejoined us. Braden tried to prepare us. "This could be grim."

It was.

Along with a complete dossier on Dr. Carthage were photos. Horrifying images of dismembered bodies stripped of their skin and inner organs. The flesh was stretched but kept supple via oils and various unheard-of treatments according to medicinal comments.

"My." Micah groaned.

"Son of a bitch." Anger clouded Braden's face as he read over the notes. "Practicing physician since his early twenties after graduating at the top of his class. Advance knowledge of all medical sciences and engineering. Mechanical specialist as well. Inventor. Is part of secret organizations well beyond the military, deep inside the Kingdom. One major unknown benefactor is

A Long Reign

supplying funds for his so-called research." Braden's words were tight with anger.

"Does it say why?" I hastily flicked through the photos and other notes. I shuddered when I remembered how the Doctor had talked about separating the skin from the bone on the day of slaughter in the field.

"No, not exactly. One can presume it's not for anything of good for the human race." Braden handed me the document. "Peruse with caution."

I scanned it for information. It was clear that he was experimenting on humans, and had been doing it for a long, long while. "I don't see anything on his age. Do you? He seemed to be getting on in years."

"Here, there's a notation that his family was well acquainted with the Lalaurie's of New Orleans. A young adolescent at the time of the 1834 fire at their mansion. The one that revealed they were torturing slaves. That can't be a coincidence. That would make him around eighty."

"He doesn't look quite that old. Pretty well preserved, I'd say. Maybe he's creating a sort of youth potion?" I offered.

"That's a possibility." Braden read over more notes. "There's anecdotal notes on formulas with blood as an important ingredient. Appears he's had a fascination with Vlad the Impaler. And the Marquis De Sade. Quite the inspiration for him." Braden sneered. "Alright, let's begin. We need to memorize everything. Every detail in the photos, every notation, word for word."

Braden put the notes and pictures in the most logical order. Some were dated. Others had pictures of the maligned physician at work, so we could take a gander at his age.

For hours, my Captain recited every line, while Micah repeated the words. By bedtime, we had immersed ourselves into the brain of a very, very sick man and our copies of his work supplied fuel for an evening fire.

The days we'd been given to recover from the Doctor's visit weren't enough.

Neither Braden nor I slept well. I tried in vain to forget the sounds of the screams and machines. The foul smell of death on the day of the reaping had ruined my appetite for quite a while.

Attempting to find comfort in each other only helped somewhat. We were just as broken as the bodies we'd seen.

11 LEARNING CURVE

New York

I remember standing with Tesla. His eyes sparkled as he spoke of how someone had made an exact replica of him.

"The plan was brilliant." His tongue clicked in his native Austrian accent. "Only that they had not expected Dorothy to notice. She's always been a good secretary. Knew I wouldn't just start working, especially since I hadn't fed the pigeons that morning." He wiped his bloody forehead again. "Ah, at last the bleeding has stopped." He handed the soiled cloth to a manservant who exited and closed the lab door behind him. "But alas, for two days I was tied up. Who knows how many secrets he stole? And for whom?"

Braden stood next to me as scientists attended to the humbot that was an exact copy of Mr. Tesla. They were undressing the machine and prepared to take it apart.

"Edison?" Braden's rich voice filled the room.

"No, someone else. His lab suffered a break-in months ago while he was traveling. He didn't think much of it at first because money was stolen from his desk. The Redcoats assured him it was probably just a vagrant." Mr. Tesla preened in a tiny mirror as he spoke while his fingers brushed a salve over his healing cut. "But after cleaning up an experiment he couldn't find a particular set of notes. It was then that he noticed documents had been taken from his library. I would suspect that someone wants the most advanced science on earth."

"It wouldn't surprise me if it was the Redcoats that stole the intel." My Captain sneered. A pop and whirring noises from the humbot interrupted our conversation. Sparks shot from the neck as the right eye burned red. An assistant pressed deep into the back side of the machine's neck. Its head popped off and rolled onto the floor with a thud.

"Looks like we found its weak point." Telsa laughed. "Decent work I suppose, but shame on them to think I could be replaced." Tesla then addressed me. "Are you sure you're ready to help us then?"

Brandon answered for me as his strong hand patted my shoulder. "She's more than ready."

But I wasn't.

The next day we finally had time alone in our lavish hotel room paid for by the Kingdom. The Colonel and his family had rooms further down the hall. Brandon started in his usual practical voice; a tone that always let me know that he truly meant business.

"We have to talk about what's going to happen when we arrive in London."

"How much time do we have to prepare?" Anxiety had been building in me since the day that Ida was killed.

"Three to four days. In the meantime, we have a while to practice, plan, rehearse, and practice again."

"What things?"

"Everything. Etiquette, tactics, but most of all, I need you to be ready, um, I mean…" He stumbled. Rarely did Braden ever falter in anything. Even when he had confessed his love for me, he was pretty stoic.

"Just say it." At this point, I was scared for what he was going to say, but I wanted to get over it in a hurry.

"I need you to be prepared to be a mistress. We are hoping to get inside the Royal Family." He looked off as he always did. It was his coping mechanism.

"You're serious?" I stood up so quickly I tripped from my chair.

"Yes, remember, we talked about this a long time ago. You'll have to be flirtatious, cunning, in order to get you into the Queen's court. We are close to certain that she is a humbot. As soon as we arrive, we'll get the best targets selected." He came away from the window.

"I'm just supposed to keep whoring myself out until we get to the right people?" I inched towards to him.

Braden tried to hide his anger, his lips furling in frustration. "Yes. And lower your voice, Lavinia."

"I'm just a fucking prostitute?" I clenched my fists.

"No, Lavinia."

"Yes, I just sleep with whoever my Captain commands me to. And then you'll just lower yourself to take leftovers when they're done? Or will you have me first to get me warmed up for them?" I grilled him. I spat out the words so fiercely that my jaw locked up.

The sting of his slap burned my cheek. "Stop it! Contain yourself."

"Oh." I slid to the floor in a crumpled mess. "Oh my God."

"I'm sorry. Lavinia, I'm sorry. For everything." He knelt beside me. I tried to resist the pull of his arms around me. "This is harsh, I know. We didn't get to choose our lives, did we? None of us did. Do you know how much I've killed? How awful that is? Remember how badly you felt after you killed that Redcoat on the Horizon? Multiply that a thousand times for me." I could feel his tears fall onto my face as he shook.

His voice trembled as he continued. "What I've had done to me? What they've done to everyone else? They have a crazy bastard that is taking slaves' skin and putting it on robots! We have to fight for all of us, Lavinia. Or we will always be stuck here in this hell on earth."

My skin crawled and my head ached. "I don't know if I can." I whimpered. "What if I refuse?"

"Look at me." Braden pulled my hair away from my face. "Lavinia, you don't have a choice."

"Now, do it again. Just like she did." Braden sat across from the bed, where male and female prostitutes embraced each other. We were in an Underground flop house that was miles away from the hotel we currently lived in.

I undressed at a snail's pace, taking off each piece of clothing with great care. "Don't forget to look at him. Register his emotions, but don't feel them. This is about power, not sex. Get him under your spell." Braden instructed. "You cannot have shame. You mustn't worry about what you look like. Control how you feel, and you'll have him. Now approach. Remember what Earl told you about being sleek like a cat."

I remembered to stand proud as I slid over to the bed but tripped over the thick ornamental rug. I blushed as I fell naked onto the bed.

Everyone but Braden burst into giggles. Yet still, he cracked a smile. "Do it again Lavinia."

The second time, I got it right. I was smooth as glass. I kissed the stranger on the bed and ran my hands over his body. It hurt me to resist looking at Braden's reaction.

"You can stop now." Braden exhaled. "That was much better. Be prepared to be like that every time. Fully aware of the space around you. Tempt them. Make them wait. Don't make it too easy. Charles, you may go."

As the male went out, Braden gave him a sack filled with money. "Now Cassie will stay. Ladies, get redressed."

I cocked a brow at my Captain. I was hoping I was finished. "And now?"

"Now, you're going to seduce her." Braden's face went blank. I hated how he could just shut down whenever he needed to. "Remember. Women are softer. Most want you to be gentle, kind. Speak sweetly. Cassie will show you."

Cassie motioned me back to the bed and held me in her embrace. Her lips tugged at my ear and tickled my neckline. She first guided my hands to her back then her breast. "Like this. Not hard. Whisper of a touch."

I stiffened. A lifetime of torture and denial of freedom had made me so afraid to do anything that felt even remotely wrong. I closed my eyes in a futile attempt to make it easier.

"Girl, you need to breathe. And don't close your eyes." Cassie stopped me. "It's harsh, but you have to see everything going on around you. They might have a guard posted outside waiting to kill you during the act. They could be an experienced spy trying to flush you out. If you're not able to do this, to act like you want them, you'll die."

Braden agreed with a nod.

"Try again. This time, I'm not leading you. Do it or you die, remember that." Cassie ordered.

"Understood." I gathered every inch of swagger I could muster and threw dignity to the wind. For the next hour, I practiced, developing a skill I hoped I'd never have to use.

I cleared my throat and whispered her name while I smoothed her lingerie from behind. I became something I wasn't. I mapped out every inch of her skin with my fingertips while sweet nothings tumbled from my lips. I was achingly slow in getting to the furry patch betwixt her legs. I lingered on her silky folds there as time seemed to freeze around us. I made eye contact until she shuddered under my gaze.

Cassie spoke up. "She's ready."

I was so awfully wicked and conflicted. Sometimes so roughly sick at what I was doing, that I thought I would vomit. I was grateful for the reprieve.

"Very well, then. You may go, Cassie." Braden proffered another sack of money. "Lavinia, you can get dressed."

Feeling strangely out of my skin, I got an idea. "Well, just maybe, I don't want to." I boldly strolled over to my Captain.

Although he allowed a miniscule grin to escape, what he said next, shocked me. "No. Get dressed, we need to hurry. You're always my wife with me, Lavinia. Remember that."

I was completely confused as I picked my clothes off the floor. Braden was next to me helping me get properly attired. Not a word was spoken as he laced my corset and helped my dress over my head. "Here, sit at the mirror." He lifted a brush from the vanity table and fixed my hair in an appropriate updo as I closed my eyes. "You can open now."

I appeared relaxed despite the conflict in my heart.

"This is what I see every day. That you are mine. You are a gift. One that, for right now, I have to share. And I cannot show that I am too jealous or too angry. You are beautiful; I have to use you as my pawn. The wealthiest and highest ranked of the court will expect this. Understand?"

"Yes."

"Good, because tomorrow, our first target is the Colonel's wife Josephine."

12 DERAILED

New York

We boarded the train from outside New York to head for the steamer that would take us to London in the early morning hours. It was about a forty-five-minute trip to the docks. It should've been an easy trip. It wasn't.

The night before was emotional and physically painful. I was tired from training and traveling. My heart and soul ached. I wanted to believe that the early evening hadn't happened. I truly only wanted one person, and that one person was as conflicted as I. There didn't seem like any other way to get inside of the Monarchy.

We had everything packed by bedtime, but I dreaded sleeping next to Braden. We hadn't said much after we entered our fancy hotel.

"Come to me, Lavinia." Braden stretched out his hand. I couldn't hold it in any longer. I burst into tears. "Shhh, come on now. You're stronger than you know. I am proud of you."

"Sure, you say that now." I blubbered.

"You are. Let's get you cleaned up." He kissed my forehead, grasped my hand, and led me into the extravagant bathroom. I was amazed at how well the entitled were allowed to shit.

Braden started the water, helped me undress, and put me in the massive tub. Soon he joined me. We spooned in the hot water. I tried desperately to relax, but my mind wouldn't stop racing.

"Let go." He washed my hair and massaged my shoulders until they should've melted. "Better?"

"Hmmm. Yes."

"Lay back against me."

I giggled. "Yes Sir."

His lips tickled my neck while making their way to tug on my ear lobe. "Let me love you." His hands came around to my breasts with a gentle circular motion. "And here." He reached down below my navel. My legs trembled as I caved to my desire.

"Bed now?"

"Yes."

Once ensconced in fluffy towels, he carried me to bed. We slept although restlessly. I heard my Captain mumble in his sleep while his brow furrowed. I wanted to wake him, but I waited to see if he could handle his nocturnal demons on his own.

Before I knew it, he shook me awake. "Good morning. The porter brought breakfast. I have to step out for preparation."

"Thank you." I rubbed my eyes.

"It'll be alright, Lavinia. Always remember that. I'll be back. Make sure you get enough to eat."

I ate at least half my meal. The eggs and sausages smelled too good to pass up. By the time I finished, Braden had come back with a bundle of roses. "You deserve these. Ready?"

"As I'll ever be." I inhaled the sweetness of flowers.

Now that the train was finally on its way, it was time for me to move as well.

"Take your time Lavinia, don't push if she resists. The Colonel and I are meeting to discuss things before we get to the docks. Make sure you are wanted. Be careful." And with a quick peck on the cheek, Braden made his way to the dining car.

I did a brief check of my make-up and smoothed over my silken black and brown striped dress as I stood. I sashayed down the aisle towards the Colonel's private car and knocked.

"Yes?" Josephine's airy voice questioned her possible guest.

"Hello." I let my warmest voice come forward as I strode into the car. "I thought you might want company now that the gentlemen are attending to business."

"Yes, that would be lovely. Come in Lavinia. Tea?" Josephine's smooth southern drawl echoed in the private car.

"Splendid." My accent had improved and apparently sounded delicious to my prey.

"I am glad you came, Lavinia. Now that I've given birth, I'm able to well, participate in more activities. And I'm glad to thank you in person for assisting in my delivery." She practically purred as she set down her cup. "Is it ever hot in here?" Josephine clearly was still interested as she unbuttoned her collar on her dress.

"Yes, it is quite warm." I soothed and sat next to her on the settee. "Let me fan you." I may have brushed too vigorously, for her hair came loose. "I am sorry. Can I fix it?"

"Please leave it down. Although I like how you're soooo helpful. Can you loosen my corset? It's uncomfortable."

"Of course." I whispered saucily in her ear as I released the buttons on the back side of her dress.

The car lurched in an alarming fashion. The train's whistle was heard, and we came to a stop. "Oh my." Josephine stuttered.

"Let me see if everything's alright." I stood just as the Colonel stepped in.

"Are you ladies okay? Apparently, there was something on the tracks. But it's already been cleared. We should be back on track momentarily."

"Well, Lavinia has been absolutely delightful." Josephine purred at her husband in a way that clearly meant that she had prurient desires.

"She could join us another time after we reach London? But for now, I must return to business." The Colonel exited with a wink.

"Hmm Lavinia dear, perhaps you could rub my neck. It's incredibly sore."

"Of course." I gently slid my fingers over her skin as she groaned.

"Men are such ruffians. Not quite knowing how to make a woman happy. Wouldn't you agree, Lavinia?"

I measured my answer carefully. "Although my Captain is

quite the gentleman, there is nothing quite like a lady's touch." I purposely sifted my hands through her tresses as I spoke.

"The Colonel had told me that the Captain said that you were extraordinary. I'd say I'd have to agree." Josephine cooed. "Please kiss me. Kiss me like a lover."

Before I could answer, the train jolted again, tossing both of us violently to the floor. I heard a loud bang and a roar that only got louder even though the train continued to move.

"Are you alright Josephine?"

"I think so." She mumbled and rolled to her side.

"Let me see what's going on." By the time I was halfway through the next empty car, the train bucked again, jumping the track and stumbling forward. The car ahead flew in sideways against mine, shattering the windows and popping me out the back side of the car. I bounced onto the mossy ground as cars buckled against each other. In a moment of hyper reality, most of the train rolled down a steep embankment in front of me, taking trees and earth with it.

"Braden!" I tried to scramble up as the train tumbled all the way to bottom of the ravine.

"Lavinia! Lavinia!" I heard the Captain yelling. For a moment I couldn't believe my ears. I limped alongside the tracks through debris and smoke. I was elated when Braden emerged unharmed with the Colonel close behind. "My God, you're safe."

"What happened?" I strained to see through the fog. The first cars and the engine unmoved by the accident.

"Where's Josephine?" The Colonel huffed while attempting to dust off his uniform. "I thought she was with you?"

"She was, but I don't know what happened. I got up to check and the train…" Wooziness enveloped me. A warm trickle ran down my leg before everything went black.

My head was pounding when I awoke. The light around me was brighter than usual.

"She's coming around, Captain!" I heard a voice, but it sounded miles away.

"Lavinia?"

I thought I heard the Captain. My focus sharpened around me. Workers and Redcoats were everywhere with tools and equipment. Out of the corner of my eye, I saw the headless body of Josephine carried out of the ravine on a stretcher by Redcoats. A man behind them gingerly carried her bloodied head in a handkerchief. Other bodies were brought up behind them, groaning in agony. "Uh oh." I muttered.

"No dear, look this way. Here, we're going to sit you up." A medic put his hands behind my shoulders. "Just a taste, a little bitter, but you'll feel better."

My leg burned in pain as I opened my mouth. I drank from the cup that they held to my lips. It was tart, but I had to trust them.

"There now." The young doctor soothed.

"Lavinia? How is she?" The Captain came to my side.

"Better. We stopped the bleeding from the slash on her leg. Another couple minutes and she would've bled out. And I think she's got a bump on the head, but no concussion. She'll need rest and stitching up. But I think she'll be alright. We need to get her into the city proper. The medic wagon is waiting."

"Captain?" The word sounded strange coming out of my mouth.

"Lavinia, just relax." Braden put his hand to my forehead as I fell back under.

Two Days Later

I was finally granted permission to leave the hospital. Being an officer's wife had its benefits. I got the best doctors and treatments that privilege could buy. Even Dr. Gideon was brought in to help.

I was lucky as a child. I remember being sick, but I never got hurt. My charm and beauty had protected me for a long, long time. Nothing could've stopped what had happened on the way to the ship.

The day before, I finally came to complete consciousness. Braden was there with affection hugs and gentle kisses. "How you feeling?"

"Better, but tired."

"Good. Don't worry. They say you'll be ready tomorrow." Braden paused as he cast a worried look around the room. He stood at the door of the hospital room and closed it. "Do you remember anything? I mean, about the accident?"

"The first time we stopped, the Colonel came into our car and said there was an object on the tracks. They got it removed. Then a loud bang. And another. I think. Why? What happened?"

Braden massaged my hand. "I have bad news. I think it was a bomb. Someone wanted to stop the train from getting to New York. I've checked all my sources with the Underground. No one knows of anything."

"Are you sure? Who would do that?"

"I don't know. The Colonel went mad at the loss of Josephine. He couldn't remember anything about the accident. He didn't even tell me what you just said about the first stop. I'm thinking the tracks were deliberately covered. While the train was stopped, they placed an explosive device under the car they thought we were in. But they were wrong; they missed it by two."

"Oh God."

"Josephine was willing to be recruited by us. I needed at least one other person on the inside. You were my bargaining chip. She wanted you. In return, Josephine would give us access to the Colonel. She also had ties to people close to the Monarchy."

"I was used to get to her?" My voice cracked.

"Yes, and I am sorry Lavinia. I know it hurts. We would've gained such a foothold with her in our ranks. I had to test you, to make sure you would follow through." Braden couldn't look at me anymore. I tried to stay calm.

"And the Colonel?"

"He's in an asylum." To my surprise, Braden moaned back at me. "We've lost our chance Lavinia. I don't know when or even if we'll get to London."

13 EBERSOL

London

"Memorize everything. We have to burn it." My Captain paced around the room uneasily. I held a scant number of pages on Ebersol's history. It was déjà vu from weeks before, but this time we had less information on a man we'd never met.

This man, known by his last name, Ebersol, was the only non-Royal Family member allowed to get close to the Queen. We had to get in his good graces as soon as possible to get into the Queen's inner circle.

Tension was rising throughout the Kingdom as Queen Victoria's new rules put more restrictions on her subjects. France and Spain were becoming the ugly stepsisters of England. The Queen's children seeded Europe to follow the Monarchy.

Groups like the Underground were starting to get a foothold in the further reaches of the Kingdom in places like East India and New Zealand.

There was pressure to have additional troops and supplies brought to the motherland to support her reign. This is how Braden managed to have us transported to England despite the Colonel's fall. Dr. Carthage was called back to England. By a brilliant stroke of luck, the decrepit doctor remembered my Captain's abundant work in Missouri. After our train derailed, word reached Dr.

Carthage that we remained in America. Within days, we were well received in London.

A Colonel from northern England, McHendrie, greeted us. "Hello Captain Davis, welcome back home. I understand it's been a while."

"Yes Sir, quite a while."

"I see you have found something you liked in the Americas." Colonel McHendrie sneered at me. He was a swarthy man with ginger colored hair and beard and a brogue that exposed his Scottish heritage.

"My lovely wife, Lavinia." The Captain waived his hand towards me in a smooth elegant fashion.

"Enchanted and delighted to meet you, Colonel." I oozed gentility.

"Ah, and the soul is as beautiful as the outside." The Colonel kissed my gloved hand. "You are quite the lucky man."

"Thank you, Sir."

"We are glad to have you here. There is much work to be done, but I am certain that with your stellar reputation, you'll be able to succeed in helping the Kingdom. For now, you'll remain at the rank of Captain, but you'll have time to set up your offices and hire staff before setting out. These two will assist you. I will leave you to get started. Good day." Two Redcoat infantry approached as he left.

My Captain whispered, "That is what is between us and the Queen. He already likes you. A good start."

We would soon find out Braden was wrong.

We settled into quarters fitting for an officer's family. I would soon find out I was the only woman in close proximity. A recent order from the Queen forbade new officers to marry. Current officers could remain married, but their wives were moved off base. Troops were intermittently allowed time away. Braden was whisked around the English countryside to observe current farming and production methods for his first full week in the country. I had a butler and a decent library. I was allowed to roam to further edges of the palace grounds.

"Listen and find out what you can. I won't be able to contact you other than through exorbitantly mushy romantic letters. Be present but not intrusive, most of all, be safe." My Captain kissed me goodbye with a look of worry.

"I will."

And so began a couple weeks of loneliness. Or so I thought. I explored as far as I was allowed. I lingered in hallways and gardens longer than I should. I heard snippets of conversation, mostly plans of Redcoat assignments.

One day as I read one of my new tomes in the garden, Colonel McHendrie approached.

"Ah, Madame Davis, how lovely to see you."

"And you, good Sir." I set my book aside.

The Colonel bore a pleasant smile. "I see you are adjusting well."

"Ah, yes Sir. I have quite the library."

"Well Madame, should you need anything, anything at all,

in absence of your husband, please do not hesitate to let me know?"

"I most certainly will." A clock tower in the garden chimed four o'clock.

"Ah, teatime. Would you like to join me for a cup?" His eyes twinkled.

"Why of course. I'd be delighted."

The Colonel caressed my hand and escorted me to an alcove outside his quarters. "Please bring tea for me and the lady." He instructed his help. "Outside well enough for you?"

"Of course." I purred.

"Times like this are precious. To be in the company of a woman these days is rare. To be in the presence of a beautiful one such as you, is rarer still." The kind words fluttered off his tongue.

"I am flattered, Sir."

"I must say, the Captain is a lucky man." He was going to continue when an attendant interrupted.

"I am sorry, Sir. I have a word for you from Ebersol."

The Colonel visibly flinched. "Excuse me Madam."

As he got up from the table, I wondered what kind of powerful man could make a military leader twitch. I made a mental note of the name Ebersol, as the Colonel and his attendant made a tense exchange in the distance. I pretended to read my book but glanced at their discord. After brief moments the Colonel entered.

"I am sorry for the delay, Madame."

"Is there something wrong, Sir? Any way I can be of service?" I encouraged with a voice that dripped with sweetness.

"Again, I am quite envious of your Captain, to have such a courteous wife. However, I will have to join you for refreshments on another date. May I have one of the men escort you back to the garden with your tea?"

"That would be lovely." Something was amiss.

"Very well. Until we meet again." He again kissed my hand and bounded away.

Braden made it back from his first brief trip with the information that now stoked the fire.

"He's dangerous. The lack of information is telling. There's secrets here." Braden grilled me as he fed the last page into flames. "And you said that the Colonel was upset?"

"Yes. Very. And he ran off, like a child late for school."

"You're certain you heard his name, Ebersol?"

"No doubt."

"He has a mechanical and military background. A possible link to Dr. Carthage. And no surprise here, skills with explosives. I wonder if he had the bomb set that crashed our train?" Braden wondered aloud. "Probably threatened by our former Colonel."

"Or his wife. Maybe she was playing both sides?"

"We'll never know for sure." Braden stood, peered out, and he began to pace. I could feel the anxiety brewing in him. "You'll need to get closer to Colonel McHendrie. But slowly. It can't be obvious. The contacts I made are weak. Depleted. They're starving, they're stuck, unable to escape. We are the best hope the Underground has had in a long time, Lavinia."

I shuddered. "I know."

Ten agonizing long years passed. Colonel McHendrie kept as much of his little power that he could. And most of it came from inroads and sacrifices that Braden and I made.

I deliberately became the Colonel's mistress. He'd never found a wife before the soldier cease marriage order was given. And he'd never liked the prostitutes that were offered. I went to his bed whenever he wanted, most times in the middle of the night. I was exhausted from continually pretending to be pleasant and accommodating while knowing that I could die at any time if discovered. I was now in my late thirties. Although still beautiful, time was not on my side.

I was completely lost without my Captain. I became hardened. Not completely heartless, but there were days that I tried desperately to remember who I was, where I'd come from, and why I was doing this. Lunches and teas with the other officers' wives were made for what parcels gossip we had to share. Most of the others were horribly bored.

Braden was gone for weeks, often months at a time. It was for more than just increasing yields. The Colonel was a competitive man. Braden was given orders to assassinate any rising soldiers in the ranks that might attempt to overtake the Colonel. Dr. Carthage turned a blind eye to the Colonel's fatal behaviors because the Kingdom's fields and factories were churning out more abundance than ever.

"These are good men Lavinia. Talented. Smart. Battle tested. In any normal militia, they'd be rewarded. Instead, I've dropped them in rivers. Buried them in newly plowed fields." A weary look crossed his face as he stripped off his uniform after a particularly long trip. "He fucks you whenever he pleases. And we're still not any closer to this Ebersol. I can't see how we can overthrow the Queen if we can't even get to the man closest to her." He paused as we heard a clatter in the hall.

A knock on the door confirmed our suspicion to be quiet. "I'll answer." Braden threw his jacket back on.

"Captain Davis, an important invitation from the palace." A Redcoat solider delivered a note they would change us forever.

The ballroom of the palace was filled with a sea of dignitaries and royalty. The stature of guests grew with each arrival announcement, until the Queen herself entered.

"Watch the others around her." Braden whispered to me as the whole room bowed to the beloved Monarch. The Queen ascended to her throne and the festivities commenced. "Her children and their spouses came in by order of birth, youngest to oldest. As we circulate, try and catch the attention of any of them." We were briefly interrupted by one of my most hated beings on earth.

"I am pleased that you could come." Dr. Carthage approached. "Colonel McHendrie said you'd be here. I believe he is entertaining ladies over to the left."

I saw that the Colonel was holding a court of three women in a corner of the immense room. His eyes met mine and I smiled while I casually flipped my fan.

"Yes, we are delighted to be here." My Captain joined the conversation.

"Ah, and your lovely wife, with the most porcelain of skin." As the doctor kissed my hand, I held back the bile in my throat and tried to press the thoughts of Ida's death from my mind.

"You are too kind." I spoke with a gentle demeanor that caught even the Captain off guard. He grinned at my deception.

"Well, I must be going. Please enjoy. It was delightful to see you again after much too long a time." The doctor strolled away.

"Was that odd? I mean, the skin. And I think more." I whispered.

"He'd peel it off you in a second." Braden drank in between his audible thoughts. "And the long-time comment. He knows we've been here forever. I'm certain he knows you're with the Colonel. It's not right. We have to keep listening. It's time to move along. Go greet who you know. We'll meet up in about an hour." Braden watched the guests and then touched my shoulder. "I still think you're the loveliest creature in the room." He kissed my cheek, we separated, and began to explore the room.

I'd never seen such ostentatious displays of wealth. I was given a gown as a gift from the Colonel that was meticulously tailored to me. I thought its radiant cobalt blue fabric and matching jewels and pearls made me irresistible. I paled in comparison to the other women in the room. I was glad Braden didn't think so.

We had been supplied sumptuous meals since coming to England, but there were gourmet displays of wealth before that made me salivate on sight. Servers brought out tray after tray of aperitifs and liquors. As I was given a glass of wine, I sensed the presence of someone behind me.

I pretended to sip and acknowledged those who passed me with a smile. Two gentlemen stopped briefly, but upon seeing my wedding ring, continued on. Others gazed at me across the room. Yet the man behind me lingered for over ten minutes. I prepared to move to another spot in the ballroom but glanced over my shoulder just as the stranger came around from behind.

"My, you are a vision of loveliness." The stranger spoke with an accent that dripped with both money and confidence. "Surely you are not alone here?"

"Hello, I'm Lavinia Davis. The wife of Captain Davis." I motioned to Braden who was deep in conversation with other officers.

"Ah yes. Your husband is quite the talented soldier. He's made stunning advances for the Kingdom. I've heard good things about him from Dr. Carthage. What a shame that the sod Colonel McHendrie gets all the credit. And you to boot." The man paused to measure the reaction of his dig. He was tall, of average build, with black and grey streaked hair. His eyes were completely black as well.

"I'm sorry, I don't believe we've met." I brushed off the insult.

"That's right, we haven't." The stranger began to walk away as the Colonel approached.

"Ebersol, I am pleased to be in your presence Sir." The Colonel grabbed the attention of the man we'd been unsuccessful in contacting. The familiar pit in my stomach burned, the sign that something was horribly wrong.

"Yes, Colonel. What a glorious evening. The Queen and

her court present for all to see." Ebersol's voice dripped with a sarcasm that the Colonel was too stupid to ignore.

"Yes, fantastic isn't it?" The Colonel waved his hand around in a giddy fashion. I pretended not to notice his garish behavior. It was obvious that he was already inebriated.

"You should select one of those lovely eligible ladies to dance with." Ebersol grimaced. "Instead of, well, cavorting with a slut in the palace."

I remained still at the second insult Ebersol had hurled at me within the space of a few minutes.

The Colonel paled and drank. "I believe that I will. Thank you, your grace for the suggestion."

I'd never seen the Colonel so ill at ease. How I managed to hide that I was shaken, I'll never know. Ebersol had not only heard of me, but he also knew of my relationship with the Colonel. I fanned myself while moving away.

"Where are you going, Madame Davis?"

"It's Madame now?" I continued to stroll in the opposite direction. I let him follow. I piqued his interest.

"I didn't dismiss you." Ebersol grunted behind me as I kept moving, albeit with caution.

"Oh, I believe you did, Sir. Twice."

"Madame Davis, please stop. I was too harsh." He slid in alongside me. "Clearly you are above such foolishness. Please come this way."

Ebersol grasped my arm and led me outside the ballroom. As we went out, I was able to glance at Braden. He gave a subtle nod and continued to drink amongst his soldiers.

We were soon outside on one of the palace's glorious balconies. The London skyline was spectacular with massive lights illuminating the immense clouds of steam that rose from the city's factories. "How amazing."

"So, you do have a heart then." Ebersol stood beside me.

"I have an admiration for beautiful things."

"As do I. You are far too gorgeous to be the mistress of a man who makes an ass of your husband."

"We do as we are told Sir. I believe that is how the game is played." I raised a brow.

"I think you've been playing far too long." Ebersol continued to engage.

"Play is the wrong word. Survive would be more appropriate."

"Ah there it is. The brutal honesty. I always wondered what the dynamic was in your household." Ebersol paused and took another long look at me. "I can change that for you, Lavinia."

"In exchange for what?" I countered. "And why?"

"I did underestimate you." His laugh echoed against the ornate stone pillars that surrounded us. "Well Lavinia, one of the Princes has taken interest in you. He makes the Queen happy, and I need to keep both of them happy. I would like for you to assassinate the Captain for me."

"Why would you kill a man that would make you look so good to the Queen?" I questioned as my heart sank.

"Why would you stay with a man that could hold you back?" Ebersol taunted.

"Stay is a relative term. My husband is an intelligent man. He is willing to do what is necessary to remain in good graces with his superiors and hopefully, to receive restitution for his work. He does not need to be in the spotlight. He would prefer to be compensated. And well at that." I retorted.

"But would you kill your husband if it meant that you could have more?"

"You know, as well as I, it is survival of the fittest. I have enough, for now. Again, my Captain has done much to serve the Kingdom and continues to move much into the coffers of the Queen. To kill him would be foolish."

"I think you might actually love him." Ebersol teased.

"I never said I had a weak heart."

Ebersol laughed. "Very well, then. Colonel McHendrie is useless. Kill him. I'll give you the means and opportunity. When it is done, you and your Captain will have a place in the court. You have my word."

Braden smoothed over my hair as I cried. We lay in bed, spent, after an evening of subterfuge. No rich food or drink from earlier in the eve could fill the emptiness.

"We finally have an in. I know you're upset. But you can do this. You must, because now we can get to the Queen. I know it's a risk, but it's our best chance. You'll manage." My captain was encouraging, but I barely slept at all.

14 ROLES

The Palace, London

Within two days of the ball, I did manage to dispose of the Colonel. It was a simple and well executed plan. I was to go to him as soon as he requested me.

"That Ebersol is quite the bastard, isn't he?" The Colonel enjoyed a cigar after our coitus. Its smoke blanketed a light haze over the elegant room.

"Yes, but he doesn't realize what he's missing." I demurred as I poured poison into the Colonel's glass with his brandy. My back was facing the bed to hide my covert operation. "Here, this will help you forget all about Ebersol." I was completely naked as I turned around and handed him the tainted drink. A perfect distraction for a man who'd made me miserable for too long.

He downed the drink in one swallow as I came away to prepare mine.

"Um, delicious. Pour me another one darling."

"Of course, dear." I barely had my hand on the bottle when I heard the choking behind me. I didn't move. I could see his reflection in the windowpane. He blushed bright red as saliva dribbled down his chin. I gazed down, poured my wine, and swilled an extended drink as I tuned out the last sounds of the

Colonel. I finished my glass and closed my eyes. What had I become?

I slipped on a robe, opened the door, and motioned to a soldier that was waiting to dispose of the Colonel. "Make sure that Ebersol knows it is done."

"Yes Madame."

I stuffed my clothing into a bag and walked to my Captain's quarters in the dark, my bare feet sifting through the dirt of the garden. I gazed up at my window. Braden stared out at me. I found it ironic how he'd always looked out the window, away from me, when things were hard. Now, when I was having one of my roughest moments, he was forced to watch me through the glass. There couldn't have been any comfort for him this time.

We'd entered a different kind of hell. The regimentation of our lives was worse than before. Braden was still holding onto his previous duties while taking on a position as assistant minister of the interior. He was grateful to still go out to the countryside for observations, for he could remain in contact with the Underground.

"No one has managed to get this far." Braden hurried to dress before being sent out. "Are you ready for tonight?"

I watched him from our new overstuffed bed. He was still so handsome. My heart pained for a better life. Or at least a simpler one.

Here, we now had everything. Our own apartment with multiple well-decorated rooms. Servants at our beck and call. The most modern of conveniences including all sorts of gadgets. Ebersol had come through with his promise. Braden reported directly to him. But our lives belonged to the Monarchy. So much for better, for tonight I would be introduced to Prince Arthur during a night at the opera. "Yes. Or at least, I will be."

Braden came to the bed as I stretched. "Can you hold on for me Lavinia? For the others?" He sat on the bed and played with my hair. "I managed to get word from Tesla. They are working on way to plan the assassination. And there is news about a machine that Ebersol has acquired. I cannot say more. You're already in enough danger, so I'm not giving you details now."

"I will. I'll do it." I would occasionally see Dr. Carthage in court. Even though Ida's death had been years before, I still wanted revenge for her.

"I love you." Braden broke. Tears streamed down his face. It was my turn to comfort him.

"We will do it. I know we can." I kissed him as I hoped that deep down, if we kept playing our parts, we could change the world outside forever.

"Your highness, Prince Arthur, this is Madame Davis." Ebersol whispered as a porter pulled out my chair behind the Prince's seat in the Royal Family's balcony.

"Delighted." The Prince didn't turn around. We were alone as other family members were attending yet a different royal outing.

I was properly seated when Ebersol winked at me and exited the box. Once the opera commenced, much to my surprise, the Prince moved in next to me.

"I find these performances quite boring. The roles are the

same over and over. I can think of many things I'd rather be doing." The Prince whispered saucily in my ear.

"So, so true." I couldn't believe the parallel to the actors on stage and to my life. I too was doing the same role over and over. And I was about to do it again as the Prince unbuttoned my dress and had me on the thickly carpeted floor of the private box.

Two hours later the curtain dropped on the stage as the Prince finished pulling his knickers up.

"Lavinia, you do not disappoint. I say, my wife is boring. She is the mother of my children. But so spoiled. And she doesn't like sex at all, not anymore. I'll send for you when I need companionship, and you will come. Anything you need, you will have. Simple, isn't it?" The Prince fixed a stray hair on my head.

"Yes. Simple." And with that I was whisked away on a private carriage back to an empty home with an empty heart that was tired of playing the same role of mistress.

"How did it go?" Braden hadn't been home for five minutes and sent the servants out. It was a week later, and I'd already been with the Prince three times. He hadn't lied when he said he wasn't getting any.

"He's, um, pretty lusty. I mean, for a man of his age."

"More than the Colonel?"

"Yes. I—I, you don't want to know." I'd never told Braden details before. I didn't want to start now. The truth was that the Prince was an excellent lover. Where the Colonel had been a selfish oaf, the Prince was generous.

"I see." Braden focused on unpacking things.

"Did you learn anything else?" I changed the subject. Conflict was brewing in the tightening of my chest.

"Have you seen Dr. Carthage or Ebersol?"

"Ebersol only in court and not every day. Dr. Carthage comes maybe once a week. Why?"

"They're reaping people here now, Lavinia. I managed to get one of my farmers promoted to here at a factory in London. He was one of my contacts remaining in the Underground. He told me that they are bringing in human skin and body parts to create an artificial army. They need a lot of equipment. It's going to take time, years at least. He said that Carthage is there three to five days a week. They've confirmed that they replaced the Queen with a humbot, now they are working on possibly replacing the whole human race."

"God." My heart ached at the thought of a machine wearing Ida's skin. "How? How is that possible?"

"It's worse. Ebersol got a hold of a special machine. One that was built by a faction of the Underground a long time ago. It has the ability to change time. I overheard one of the dock workers talking about a peculiar looking car that was brought in from America. It's here on the palace grounds. I would assume near Ebersol's quarters. Can you imagine, between the two of them, how much power they have? With the robotic Queen acting under their control?"

My stomach churned. "What about the Underground?"

"There's been a resurgence. More resistance. I think that's why they've stepped up the reaping. They wouldn't have to control a human population if they had humbots in their place. Micah and

Dr. Gideon have escaped Underground." Braden had a terror in his eyes I hadn't seen before. "Lavinia, whole towns across the Kingdom are disappearing."

It was past midnight when I left the Prince and headed for the wing that supposedly housed the experimental labs of Dr. Carthage. The timing for satisfying the Prince's needs couldn't have come at a better time.

It had been a few years since we'd made it into the palace. Every chance, every spare moment was spent finding out what we could on the supposed time machine and Dr. Carthage's cannibalistic experiments.

Braden would meet with Ebersol every two weeks. My Captain wasn't trusted enough to know about the time machine. But he could peer through files that were open. He would eavesdrop on every conversation everywhere he went, whether it be a farm on the far reaches of the Kingdom to Redcoats at the docks who received immense unmarked parcels that tended to smell poorly. My Captain was finally able to discover that a sample of these parcels was sent every week to a certain room in the very wing wherein I was standing.

The soldier on watch at the end of the wing had gone on a break to the facilities. Once he'd vacated his post, I ran for the room, numbered fifty-seven. I listened as long as I could for any sounds before opening the door. I only heard my heart pounding as if it would leap out of my chest.

I slipped in with panther like stealth, peering at the insides. There was a regular office with an ornate desk and decorative lamps. I got fully inside to investigate further. There were two other doors. Gratefully one was a closet with linens and medicines. The other led to a spiral stairway. I bustled downward into the long-rumored lab. Various vials and jars lined a multitude of shelves against exposed brick walls. I then saw what I had dreaded most. The stretched skin from a human leg with the toes still attached.

I gingerly stepped forward. The skin had been tattooed in a corner by the knee. Certain areas had been marked off and appeared to be treated with chemicals. Still other sections were attached to screws and bolts.

I'd seen enough. I jumped up the stairs and shut the lab door behind me. I was leaving out the office door when I heard Dr. Carthage's drunken voice echoing in the hall. I had no idea what was behind the other doors. The guard may have been back at the other end. I was trapped.

I decided to wait outside the doctor's door as he approached. I was lucky, he was barely coherent. "Ah Lavinia, is that you?"

"Why yes, I wasn't feeling well and thought you might be able to help?" I was as sweet as the ripest pear.

"Well, I'm sure I—I have something." He stumbled against me and hiccupped. His hand brushed my face as he nearly fell. "Oh dear. Oh dear, Lavinia. You have such creamy, lovely ivory skin." The backside of his fingers grazed my face. I froze. "You manage to stay out of the sun. That makes your skin, so, so, pretty."

"Well, I, uh, actually feel much better now. I think I just need to rest." In my mind, I prayed that he wouldn't remember this exchange. As I prepared to leave, he grabbed my wrist.

"Come on now. Where you going?" He slobbered. "Not

without a proper goodbye kiss."

I exhaled as he kissed my hand. "Well thank you, doctor."

"Good night, dear." He opened the door to his office and almost fell in. I walked off and didn't look back.

"God, Lavinia." Braden held me as I cried.

"I swear I had visions of him ripping off my skin." I'd had an insidious nightmare. It had been three days since I'd found the lab. Braden had come home that day and we'd finally had a night to catch up. I had slept fitfully. Braden held me after my night terror.

"If we can hang on, maybe three or four more months, we'll have a plan in place. The Queen's Jubilee will be a huge distraction. If we can take her down, in public, it could be a signal for all the factions to rise up. If we can get them to take part, to rebel, we should be able to change history."

"Another role to play." I muttered as I fell asleep.

15 INFILTRATION

A Few Months Later

"Ebersol has requested your presence at the palace, Lady Davis." A Redcoat handed me the invitation. It was two weeks before the Queen's Jubilee.

My life had radically changed again. The Prince had no desire to see me. There were echoes that his wife was unhappy. There was no comment from the Queen. "Try not to worry about it Lavinia." Braden prepared yet again for another trip. "I think they are preparing for the oldest to take over. The Queen could live past one hundred. But they want everyone to see how well she is now. And at least, now you have time to train."

There was very little word on anything but the Jubilee. My Captain was given the title of Lord. Now I was a Lady, but a Lady who had fallen so far from grace, that I feared I could never salvage any remainder of my life, save working for the Underground.

The price of preparation was high for everyone. Braden was rarely home. When he was, he was continually taking commands from Ebersol, although most of the communication was through notes and transmissions. We both suffered hideous nightmares. We clung to each other when we could as a substitute for true slumber.

The Kingdom bore the strain of years of stripping its supplies. Lands were barren from over farming. People vanished on a constant basis. Sometimes rounded up by troops and put into different work camps. Even the wealthy elite began to lose servants and the finer things. The factories in London were in over drive, belching out huge billows of thick smog that clouded the skyline at all hours of the day and night. It was like a disease that infiltrated a body and was eating that person away from the inside. And that illness was contagious, it spread like negativity and gossip from which no one could hide. Dr. Carthage had never been true to his Hippocratic oath.

The cure was in the remainders of the Underground. Their numbers had grown, but they had trouble hiding in plain sight. Braden had managed to turn hundreds of Redcoats around the globe to our side, and in a stroke of luck, one of them was a technician that was able to break into the palace's transmitter. We could now get word of all basic business of the palace. Braden and I were the only links to the Royals. They kept their secrets close to the vest. We still strove for answers.

When Ebersol called for me, I attempted to remain calm. "What do you think?" I inhaled and asked my only love. My one remaining link to humanity.

"You have to go. Agree to whatever he says but don't make it easy. Make yourself valued. We'd surely be gone by now if he didn't have a reason. I have orders to be back in two days." Braden finished his packing and held me close. "Continue to train. You have your boots?"

"Yes. And the dress for the Jubilee is made. I had it sent out to the address you gave me, so I can prepare unencumbered."

"Good. If I don't return, you must follow through. Once the Queen dies in the open, there will be mass hysteria. The Underground will take over. There should be enough people to overrun the Kingdom and start over. We just, we—"

"I know. We may not make it."

"Ah Lavinia. I'm enraptured as always." Ebersol met me in his private apartment.

"Thank you for the invitation, Sir. Although I am quite curious as to what you'd like to discuss with me today."

"Please come to the dining room." His arm slid through mine with the ease of a snake. He said nothing else as we approached the table which was filled with curious delights. There were no servants in attendance. Ebersol seated me himself. "There now, in place like a proper lady."

"I try to believe that I still am." The admission passed my lips unexpectedly but reaped amazing results.

"Lavinia, how harsh you are. One shouldn't be critical of themselves. Especially one as rare as you." He poured wine for both of us. "A toast to one of the true ladies on the planet."

My mouth was agape but I managed to sip then speak. "Thank you." Emotionally, I tried to prepare for what vile verbiage he'd sling at me next.

"Surely you know, I am pleased with your loyalty."

"I have tried my best Sir. All for the good of the Kingdom."

"You have managed to align yourself with the best of people. A husband that adores you. A man you'd do anything for. How blessed he is to have you. I see the way that you cling to him. How you look at him still. You are quite the pair. I must confess, I am envious of the happiness you have made last over quite some time. And all this, despite having to satisfy the needs of others who could definitely better serve you. Please, enjoy." He pointed towards the hearty plates before me.

I thought, if I was going to die from poisoning, at least it'd be from delicious vittles. I tentatively filled my plate.

He chuckled. "Go on, it is all clean, untainted. I admire your intelligence as well as your beauty. One does not make it to their forties without such careful consideration of all around them. You, my dear, see everything." He dug into his food with the passion of a lover.

I attempted to do the same. My usual artificial layer of coolness was hard to maintain in my mounting fear of the maniac I was dining with. "Thank you, I am flattered."

"What do you see in your Captain, well, your Lord now?"

"Kindness. He has always been kind to me."

"What? By sending you out to fuck other men? That's far from kind." And there was the zing.

I continued to eat although my appetite was long gone. The conversation was officially rigged. "We've spoken about this before, have we not? Survival is simple. You do what is necessary."

"I wouldn't have." Ebersol snatched a deliberately, sexual

bite of his meal.

"Really?" I tilted my chin and sipped my wine. I was genuinely curious.

"Women are hard to trust. Especially beautiful ones. There is always an agenda." He ate another exotic bite. "But you. I think you're different. You still go back to your Captain, your Lord. That commitment is rare. Especially after earning the attention of a prince."

"Maybe. But love makes you do silly things."

"And love is silly? In your case I think not."

"I would have to agree." I tried not to think of Braden. Despite our foibles, we had a bond. One that would certainly be broken by death.

"I have yet, in all my life, been able to find a gentle woman such as yourself. That is why I've remained alone and why I put up such a cruel façade. Again, I am jealous of your ability to love." A long sip of wine passed through his lips before he spoke again. "Do you think you could be that way for me?"

I was totally unprepared for this. "I—"

He stood and came to my side. "You don't have to give me a perfect answer. But I, a man who holds the keys to the Kingdom, and will soon be its ruler, will need a Queen by my side. Can't you see that you are the most befitting of the task?"

I saw the hollow eyes of a madman, completely aghast. My hand stopped, frozen halfway from my plate.

Again, he moved to the other side of the room and played a phonograph with the snap of a switch. A lovely waltz echoed through the room. "Please, dance with me." Before I could respond, he jerked me from my chair mid-bite. My fork flung to the floor with a clatter.

"Say nothing, enjoy the music." His hand pushed deep into my low back and around my waist. There was no escaping as we twirled around the room. I only managed to survive the entrapment by closing my eyes and pretending that he was Braden. Finally, the music stopped.

"You my dear, are bewitching. Come." He again tugged me away. We burst through his bedchamber doors. "Be mine, say it. Renounce your husband."

"You'll kill him anyway?" Was all I could think of.

"If you like. But I can see that it won't erase the memory of him. So, I'll let him live. That is, if he could stand to see you in my presence every day and not want to commit suicide. Besides, I still need a good man under me. And for eternity, a good woman."

Ebersol lunged at me and threw me on the bed for a passionate kiss. I had to cave to his desires, despite the rising vomit in my throat. My hair comb fell away in a flourish as he yanked on my hair. I gasped for air.

"Come now. Show me the naughtiness that the Prince bragged about." His hands were up my skirt and pulling at the ties on my bloomers.

"I can't. I can't." I sat up and heaved incredible sobs. I smeared my maquillage in a vain effort to stop crying.

Ebersol ceased his assault. "You do love him, then, don't you?" His voice was a low, husky growl.

"Of course, I do." I rearranged my skirting and slid from

the bed, wondering if he'd shoot me in the back if I ran. I picked up my favorite hair comb, one that Braden had made especially for me and headed for the door.

Ebersol stood and straightened his jacket. "My, what a test you have passed, my lady. Now there is no doubt in my mind that I must have you at my side. You demonstrate such strength, such fortitude. See, even you understand that you have no choice in the matter, although you can pretend that you do. After the Queen's Jubilee, you will be mine. I always get what I want. But I will give you one reprieve. If you are with me now, and promise to be my bride, I will keep the Captain in good standing and alive. If not, I kill you both. I mean, why should I have to wait for anything?"

I slid down in the doorway. I was completely defeated. If I died, everyone else would. The world would fall away. A single sacrifice could save us all. I dared to bargain. "If I come willingly, may I have a few days with my Captain? Please, I beg of you."

Ebersol snickered then snapped. "I'll allow it. But you give yourself to me now." It was as if the voice of Satan echoed in the bed chamber.

I pushed off from the floor and undressed in front of him. I shut off my mind as I allowed him to have my body.

"Where have you been?" The doorman's questioning jolted me awake. How different today was from that evening when I had fallen in love with my Captain. That memory had kept me alive. I went to those thoughts several times daily. Otherwise, I am certain that I would've died. Braden's love was barely sustaining me.

I flicked my fan over my face. It was ungodly hot,

especially in full royal attire. "Your highness has been waiting for you." He hissed and sneered.

I raised an eyebrow and took the hand of the butler. I was ushered up two flights of stairs in the palace. I was not royalty, but my husband was now fully embraced as Lord Davis. I had done much to earn my place on the dais beside him this day. Unspeakable acts that made me sick and disheartened in daylight and haunted me with night terrors as I attempted to sleep. I was far from a proper lady, but as planned from the start, my beauty had caught the eyes of men, including a prince. Being a preferred lady of the court, so to speak, had brought me here.

As my Lord prepared to join me at the balcony for the Queen's Centennial Birthday celebration, Brandon was dragged away in an awkward scuffle. I dare not look at him. Somehow, they found out. They knew.

A light wind caused the curtains to billow in the sunlight as my emotions crashed. I gave a pretend smirk to Ebersol and the Prince. I let them think that I was happy that my espoused had been caught, while my heart pounded in my ears. What was taking the Queen so long?

Finally, she entered, the crowd in ecstasy as she sat on the throne on the balcony.

I had my shot at last. And as expected, they pulled me away, their fingers burying deep into my skin. My boots dragged thick black marks onto the well-polished floors. As they drug me, just as it happened with the faux Tesla, sparks, assorted gears and springs sprouted from the opening that I had dug into the nape of Queen Victoria's neck with my carefully crafted hair comb. The shock of electricity had run through the metal of the throne and stung in the tips of my boots. I had sprung forth into the sunlight in front of millions to assassinate.

Shouts echoed in my ears. As did the roar and screams of the crowd as the mechanical Queen blew up on the balcony and her head crashed below. My hair fell onto my face, obstructing my view, as the Redcoats dropped me to the floor to assist those royals around me. In that moment, I hoped to escape as the world blurred. I hoped that the truth had been revealed to all.

But just as I scrambled to my feet and prepared to run, I saw my former lover prince. I was now a traitor. He stood incredibly still with a furled lip and glared at me. An icy chill ran through my veins as I noticed his right eye had the same red glare as Tesla's humbot. The last thing I remember seeing was Ebersol standing over me, his face red with rage.

16 BACK FORWARD

A Farmhouse, Fifty Miles West of St. Louis, Missouri
October 1895

I awoke with a jolt. I sat straight up in bed, clad only in the darkness. I heard a floorboard creak and the hiss of a match. I held my breath.

"Don't worry Lavinia, it's me." Braden's face was aglow with the match. He snatched an oil lamp from a table in the room and lit it.

I recognized familiar furnishings, but I was certain I hadn't seen them in years. Dizziness overcame me while I grasped the side of the bed. "What happened? Where are we? Didn't we train here?" My mind was a jumble, and I was cold.

"Yes, yes." He sat on the bed next to me and covered me with a blanket. In my time travel confusion, I didn't even realize I was naked.

"Thank you." I blushed.

"Take deep breaths. I have to get you up to speed in a hurry."

"But we stopped them, didn't we? I mean we at least got the Queen?" I sputtered as he put his arm around me, blessed that he always made me feel safe no matter what.

"Yes, but, um, things changed. Several times over." He didn't sound happy.

"I didn't dream all that, I mean, getting to London, pulling off the assassination?" Fear rose in my gut.

"No but listen. We don't have much time. I have to return the Traveler, the time machine." His voice cracked.

"Now?" I clutched his arm as if I could stop him. "You found it? That's how we got here?"

"Yes, now. I have to go back." He moved hairs from my face as he always liked to do.

"I need to get ready?" I hadn't a clue where I would go.

"No, you have to stay."

"Why did you bring me back? I don't understand— "

"Lavinia, I can't explain, I mean..." He paused. A pained expression crossed his face. "Because you don't make it."

"What?"

"You don't survive. In fact, it's possible you've been killed in two scenarios. Before you took out the Queen, I was taken away. I managed to break free because you were the perfect distraction. Just as we had always planned. I hid as they dragged you off during the chaos. I watched them shoot you. Ebersol was there. I couldn't wait any longer." He stuttered and wiped tears from his face.

"I got incredibly lucky, I managed to take cover in the same room where they stored the Traveler. I couldn't believe how arrogant and stupid they were. There were construction plans and operation details right there."

"I couldn't live without you. I made an incredible gamble, I realized Prince Arthur was a humbot. All of the royal family were. I went back only minutes and changed our plans. I made quick work of the Prince before he left his bedroom, but I couldn't get to Ebersol. You were doing the same in the Queen's sitting room as she prepared for her ceremony. You wouldn't remember this. I only changed time for five minutes in order to get you back here."

"If we stopped them, why couldn't we stay?"

"I did it only to get the Traveler back in good hands. But I have to return it closer to creation. Ebersol is part of a deeper conspiracy called the Mass." A sad look crossed his face.

"Because of our journey, the Mass was able to trace back to a crucial juncture of your recruitment, about ten years in. Which is where we are now. I'm taking a chance because I believe that they had you killed a couple days ago." I watched the tension in his neck as he swallowed hard.

I shuddered. I wasn't supposed to be here at all. "But how?"

"I think they made a copy of the Traveler and he came back here as soon as they could. The only way to stop it is to kill Ebersol in a time zone before he finds out that the original traveler even exists. That would be before 1899, in St. Louis. There are people there that can help. I can't say much more, it'll pose a threat to you if you know too much or if I didn't change time enough. I have to go. I will hopefully find you in the future." He stood up abruptly as my heart broke.

"But won't this pose a kind of wrinkle in time?" My voice cracked.

"I honestly don't know. This was my only solution to save you. To save us. I love you, Lavinia." He leaned over and gave me the warmest kiss.

"You know I'll be an advanced age by then." I smiled ruefully.

"Well, I like older women. Besides, who knows how old I'll really be?" He laughed as he pulled items from his pocket. "Take these." He handed me an exquisite pocket watch and a coin unlike any I'd seen before. "The coin has an address engraved on the edge, 47 Henrietta St. And a number on one side, 723. Try to make it to that address. It's in London, around 1898, I think. And you might want to put clothes on before you go."

I raised a brow. "How—"

"Don't ask. Just be ready. Ready for anything, anytime. I have no idea what the world might be like. Now, or in the future. It could be radically different. It will be changed." He appeared so disturbed that I couldn't even fathom what he'd seen as of late.

"Stay alive. For me?" I whispered.

"I'll do my best. Until tomorrow my dearest. I love you." He kissed me once again and dashed out the door before I could respond.

I heard a pop and a bright flash like lightning brightened the room. I knew he was gone. I finally cried. For the first time in forever, I mourned. I wept for my friends and family that were destroyed. I cried for a world that hadn't known peace. But most of all, I cried because I felt so very alone and had no idea of what the future would bring.

I didn't sleep at all that first night. Instead, I gathered up what seemed to be familiar from what I'd known as a safe house, a couple miles outside of the village, and far outside of St. Louis. I remember staying there when I was twenty-one. I picked up the oil lamp that Braden left behind. There was more food than I remembered, sacks full of dried vegetables and jerky. But there was dust on the windowsills, on the table in the rudimentary kitchen, and on the pantry shelves. When I lifted the food sacks, there were clear spots. Apparently, this wasn't a permanent residence, but maybe I could make it work. Save my lamp and starlight, it was dark.

For the next weeks, I was out of place, even though my circumstances due to the time change were much better. Or as I should say, time changes. There was at least one more, for one moment I was standing near a creek where I'd set up camp to fish, the very next minute I was back in the safe house.

I went into the village every day. It now had a name, Eureka. On that first day, I waited just outside of town to observe people. I was shocked to see colorful garb. Many ladies were very well dressed. Most people chatted amongst each other openly in the street. Not one was a soldier.

The buildings were grand. There was an opera house and an open market bustling with shoppers. Food was piled up in the stalls. From the colors of the trees, it was harvest time. Trains came and went on a regular basis and all kinds of people rode them.

The wind blew a large paper with words printed all over it by me. It was much like the newspapers I'd seen only the wealthiest people of the Kingdom have. I snatched it up and hustled to the cabin. It was dated October 5th of 1895.

Like those papers, it was filled with information, and I read every word. But unlike the ones I'd seen in my previous life, ordinary people were featured. Shops advertised their wares. It said who was born, who got married, who died, and that the community was having a harvest bonfire that Saturday by a church and school.

For the next week, I stayed on the fringes of town. I found old ladies' dresses in ash pit to replace the hunter's wear from the cabin. I cleaned, modified, and mended them. I didn't want it to look like I nicked garbage. I listened to how people talked and what they said. If anyone passed, I grinned and didn't speak unless spoken to. I also found a battered old trunk behind the rail depot. If I was going to get somewhere, I had to look like I'd come from somewhere else.

I decided to hold onto my world capital accent. Although now London was just the capital of England and its remaining territories. I went to the general store and tried not to be in awe of the items available for purchase. The owner greeted me with a genuine smile.

"Hello Madam. Is there something I can help you with?"

"Well, yes. I'm new in town." My accent rolled richly off my tongue as I picked a fresh newspaper off a table just inside the door.

"Yes, I can hear that. Old English, from the land of the old redcoats." He continued to grin until my face soured at the word redcoats. "I didn't mean to insult you Ma'am. After all, they haven't been called that around here since the Revolutionary War."

"No matter." I needed to remain calm, I still didn't know much. "What I do need is work." People had money now, and they earned it.

"Well, you sound educated. The school marm needs help. More children pouring into town all the time." He gazed down at the newspaper. "Can read and write I guess?"

"Yes, Sir. And maths too."

"Well, the school is right next to the church. I think they'd be delighted to have someone of your caliber there."

"Thank you kindly." As I prepared to go, I realized I didn't have money for the paper. I prepared to set it down when the clerk spoke up.

"Welcome to Eureka, Madam?"

"I'm Lavinia. Lavinia Davis." I figured I'd take the Captain's last name. I shook the proprietor's hand and gave my warmest smile. I enchanted him.

"I'm Peter Tiller, and please, just take that paper. A little welcome to town gift."

"Much appreciated Sir and have a lovely day."

As luck would have it, the schoolteacher was in desperate need of help. So much so, that they were offering free room and board through the church convent next to the schoolhouse. It was time to evacuate the cabin, hunting season was in full swing. I didn't need to be discovered there.

The school had a library, and I devoured all the books in short order. I read history first as I held the strange coin in my hand, turning it over and over while trying not to pine for my Captain. At night, I had the most realistic dreams ever. I wasn't sure what was real from my past or imagined from my subconscious.

The world as I'd known it was completely changed. The North had won the Civil War. Queen Victoria remained alive as a human and a decent one at that. There were new machines and equipment invented all the time, but not all of it was accessible to everyone just yet. Still, people had money, people had things, but most of all people had hope.

I made friends but remembered to keep my distance. That proved to be vital, for weeks later I passed a black woman in the street. She eyed me in a strange fashion. I smiled back.

"Excuse me Ma'am, but I hate to ask, but, uh, I was wondering if I knew you?" The woman was plainly dressed and uneducated. She had a pleasant face, but it was her almond shaped eyes that I recognized. I had to ignore the rush of happiness that welled in me. I realized I'd run into Ida.

"I'm ever so sorry. I'm from England. I've come to help out before returning. I teach at the school."

"Aw shucks, I am sorry Ma'am. You just looked like a lady me, and my Sissy used to know. We was friends as childrens."

"How nice. And your sister lives here?" I gently pried.

"Naw, she was able to leave to up North after the Civil War. She got a nice family she works for. She come on down every year. She all I got, so I reckin' I might go move there."

"And what happened to your friend?" I couldn't escape my curiosity.

"Ma'am, it was sad. She was a smart lady, was a lot like you, but she died. They think she got hit by a late-night train. They buried her, you know, over by the church. I kinda hoped she was

A Long Reign

back. But I'm sorry, I didn't mean to stop you from your business. And I gotta go. Work for a farm, just came into town to help get supplies."

Just then, a black man hollered from across the street. "C'mon Ida, we gots to go."

"I'm a comin'." She called back. "Well, it was nice meeting you Ma'am."

"You too." I breathed a sigh of relief as she left. The women I'd known as sisters were both alive, free, and well. It was then I realized that there was no gallows and rules in the town square.

I went to the cemetery later that day. As I walked amongst the stones, I wondered how many children would never be born. How many were. And right before I was ready to leave, I found my headstone. My Captain had been right. Ebersol had found and disposed of me.

By next spring, most of the town's children were put to work on farms. I wasn't needed at the school anymore. It was a sign that I should earn enough to get to London. Besides, time had shifted so much that I had no idea what else might have happened in my past that hadn't been buried with me.

A wealthy rail operator needed a tutor for two older female children in Boston. He was impressed with my talents and asked me to accompany his family to London on a business trip that could take several years. It was easy to tell him yes.

London 1898

The cobbler shop on Henrietta Street was like any other:

simple awning, gray painted trim, and windows grimy from the industrial soot of London. The bells on the door rang pleasantly as I entered. I pretended to look around the shop as the cobbler came from behind a thick woolen curtain.

"Well, hello, Madam. How may I help you today?" He was perfectly collected. Not a single hint of any impropriety.

"I have a pair of shoes that need new heels. I was wondering how much you would charge to repair them?" I gave my widest, most courteous smile while attempting to tone down my upper crust accent that Braden had helped me cultivate long ago.

"Six shillings."

I had hoped to hear him say a crown, because that's the kind of piece my Braden had given me. I managed to hide my disappointment. "Thank you, Sir, I will bring them around tomorrow if that would be alright?"

"Certainly Madam. We're open until five today though if you'd like to come back?" His eyes twinkled as if to encourage me.

"Well, I'll see if I'll have time later this afternoon." I needed to play coy. I had no idea of what or who I was dealing with. I decided to throw a lure. "Is there a place where a lady could get a good cup of tea?"

"Yes, just across the street is a decent café. Good scones too, Miss."

"Thank you, Sir. Very much appreciated. Good day."

"Good day, Madam."

I strolled out the door, not too fast, not too slow. I had to play along. I crossed the street with the precise amount of caution and headed into the café. Despite bustling traffic a block away, the café was only half full. A clean-cut, middle-aged man pushed his newspaper aside at the counter.

"Please seat yourself Madam. A server will be with you shortly."

"Thank you." I chose a seat close enough to the doorway. I needed to see out the window. A ginger haired young man finished helping a distinguished older woman near the back of the café and then arrived at my table for my order.

"Good day Miss. Tea and anything else?"

"Yes, black with milk and honey. And I hear the scones are delicious." I decided to hasten the game.

"Very well Miss." He was swift in turning his ticket in at the counter. He brought a waiting order to the woman in back. With a sidelong glance I noticed a longer exchange than normal. I strained to listen but couldn't hear anything over the voices of others.

Why was it hard still, even after all these years, to pretend not to notice what was going on around me?

Suddenly my timepiece moved. In all the time I'd possessed it, it had never done anything but keep time. I couldn't hide my surprise. I flinched. I pretended to adjust my napkin as it continued to dance about in my pocket. I slipped my hand discretely under the cloth and wrapped my fingers around the pocket watch. It finally stopped. Its warmth tickled my palm. Fearing it would explode, I brought it out and feigned checking the hour.

It buzzed like a bee again, but this time, it also lit to an incredible green hue. I snapped it shut just as the server arrived with my tea and scones.

"Anything else, Miss?" He set down the tea pot and cup with too much precision for a petite café like this one.

"No, thank you." I split and buttered my scone when I noticed the older woman approach my table.

"May I join you?" She wore a rose-pink colored dress with a matching hat. "You are alone?" She had a smooth accent. Definitely elitist.

"Please do." I waved my hand towards the open chair which she eased into with the elegance of a swan.

She motioned to the server, and he procured her refreshments and brought them to the table. "I'm Madame Bartlett, pleased to meet you." She extended a pink gloved hand.

"Lavinia James, likewise." As we shook hands, I noticed she had an extraordinary grip for a woman of a certain age.

"Pleasantries aside then." With deft flicks of her fingers, she removed her gloves and started to add sugar to her tea. "Moments ago, your timepiece shuddered, did it not? Perhaps give off a strange glow?" She peered over her cup as she began to sip her drink.

"Perhaps." I equaled her cool demeanor as I nibbled on my treat.

"And this pocket watch does not belong to you?" Her words were as sharp as the knives on the table.

"It was given to me." I spoke as plainly as possible. I didn't need to lie.

"But that doesn't mean it belongs to you now, hmm?" She sipped again with her ice blue eyes glaring through the steam of her tea. I remained silent and locked in my gaze as I bit into my food.

She tried another tactic. "You know you've been discovered. You can either play nice or you can expire. Which would you prefer?"

"I've already died before. Twice actually. Let's play nice then." With a raised brow, I succeeded in earning her trust.

"Well then, Miss James. How did you procure the piece?"

"Again, it was given to me."

"Come now." She growled. "By whom?"

"An officer of the Redcoat Army." I know I managed to get under her skin as she visibly paled.

"Hmm." She poured more tea. I could almost see her mind whirling around. "When? Surely you don't mean during the Revolutionary War of the Americas? And did they give you anything else?"

"How kind of you to ask." I smirked. "At the end of the Civil War. And yes, this." I pulled the very special crown from my bag.

"May I?" With an inquisitive turn of her head, she reached for the coin.

"Say please." I pretended to whine.

"Pease. And stop it. I know what this is." She plucked the

crown from my palm and squinted at the engraved side and numbers. "Finish your tea." She barked. "We have shoes to fix."

17 THE PAST NEVER HAPPENED

A Castle Outside of London, November 1895

"Welcome to the London Society Mrs. Davis. I'm Dr. Eliza Jacobson. You may call me Dr. Jake." A statuesque woman of mixed heritage greeted me. She had Asian eyes and creamy light brown skin. A well gathered nest of braids framed her face and was topped with a vivid blue and green fascinator that matched her stunning dress. "Thank you, Director Graham." She spoke to Madam Bartlett. I gathered Bartlett wasn't her real name.

"Delighted to meet you, Dr. Jake." My manners were flawless. I stood as high as my new lady's dress boots would allow.

"Dr. Jake will take it from here. Again, Mrs. Davis, our conversations can be shared with Dr. Jake, but no one else. There is much to learn, much to adjust to, after such a long journey." Madam Bartlett informed. "My true title is Director, as I'm sure you've deducted at this point. Any word of impropriety will reach me, I'm sure you understand?"

"Of course." I gave my most haughty smile.

"Come then, we have much to discuss." Dr. Jake led me through an enclave into glorious hall of a castle that had survived centuries of uprisings. Another meeting, more questions. I was tired of these new Discussions as they called them. But all of that changed in an instant as she continued. "Your Senior, Captain Davis, has been informed of your arrival and should be back from an Engagement in about seventy-two hours. In the meantime, you'll be assigned to me for training." A rush of satisfaction unlike any other came over me.

We paused in the hall. "Ah now, there's the real Mrs. Davis." Dr. Jake grinned. "Remember, there are rewards for your service, Mrs. Lavinia."

The first couple days in the Society were near blissful. I was pampered, given time to rest, and adjust. Once properly acclimated, I met with the Director and my Senior Member, Dr. Jake. To earn my trust, they'd showed me pictures of Braden with the Traveler. My arrival had been expected.

"It's incredible that you survived." Director Graham continued to make notations as a newfangled transmitter recorded every detail of my adventure. "Your story and the Captain's align precisely. His Engagement was to assassinate Dr. Carthage and Ebersol and return the Traveler to St. Louis. I am pleased to say that has been accomplished in a most dignified and quick fashion."

"Thank God." I couldn't hold my excitement. The Director smiled at my reaction. My stomach finally settled.

"He is to be back in London tomorrow and we will meet and discuss further opportunities then. Thank you for your service to the Society. I believe Dr. Jake has updates for you as well."

"After a thorough exam, I can confirm that at some point you were sterilized, but I'm not certain how. You still have the scar from the slash on your leg during the train derailment. I'm going to run further tests, but you are indeed healthy despite what damage was done to you." An agonized look crossed Dr. Jake's face. "My only concern is that you must know that your past has been completely erased. We still don't know the full effects of travel on your bodies, or history for that matter. I am working with Members in St. Louis to further investigate what little we can. If it is of any comfort, we do believe that you and the Captain most likely saved the world from complete destruction. We have revised your histories and again, you will have plenty of time to adjust. You may come to me at any time should you need to unload your thoughts, feel stressed, or anxious."

"Well done, Mrs. Davis. I believe that we will soon be calling you Lady Davis, as you and the Captain have earned your titles. Please rest and prepare for you husband's return."

"Thank you." I still couldn't believe I was here, in an amazing world.

The Next Evening

"The past never happened, Lavinia. None of it, since an obscure point during the Civil War. There's no worldwide tyrannical Kingdom, no mass slavery. No draws. No humbots. No more Dr. Carthage or Ebersol." My Captain cried as we held on to each other. "I can't tell you exactly how, but I disposed of those bastards. And I destroyed the second Traveler."

"You did it." I grinned despite the tears that fell upon my cheeks.

"I couldn't have done it without you." Braden looked directly into my eyes for the first time without fear or having to cope with embittered emotions. "I will never allow that to happen again. No one will ever touch you again so long as I'm alive. I love you."

"I love you too, darling." That night we'd slept better than we had in more than thirty years. Well, thirty years of our old life.

In the coming days, we made love, unfettered by interruptions of violence, fear, and exhaustion. We christened every inch of our private spaces.

I delighted in the softness of his hair in my hands while he thrust deep inside me and the sounds of pleasure we could make without worry of discovery. Experiencing the joy of being deliciously naughty, loving, and romantic with the one man I wanted to spend eternity with, finally freed me from the terrors of my past.

We touched each other's scars, physically and internally. The melting of our bodies healed our wounded souls.

Wilson Manor, The Society Grounds, St. Louis, MO

"More tea?" Leeds, our temporary butler, served an exquisite afternoon meal in a garden outside our temporary home, a lovely Victorian painted lady.

"Yes please." Braden enjoyed a second sandwich. I buttered my third scone.

"Lord Wilson will send for another Discussion with Dr.

Harrington about your coming duties. But in the meantime, he'd like for me to make certain that your arrangements are to your liking?" Leeds paused.

I gazed at the immense greenery around us and couldn't suppress my smile. I was satisfied.

"Lady Davis and I are good for now, thank you." Braden touched my hand. He waited until Leeds trotted away and into the manor before continuing. "Can you believe all this?"

"Barely." The dessert melted in my mouth.

"A complete fresh start. New lives. Anything we want. Of course, a small price to pay in return for our efforts."

"Um, yes. A little work. But manageable." I took another long draw from my cup. It was simply the most fragrant and delightful tea I had ever tasted. "We are the only witnesses to the tragedy that could've happened. It makes perfect sense."

"Yes, to live in such splendor, with my wife, as Guardians of the Traveler, sounds like a fair trade to me." Braden leaned over and kissed me without a care in the world.

THE END

BOOKS FROM VICTORIA L. SZULC

More works (and future releases) by Victoria L. Szulc:

The Society Trilogy (a steampunk series, revised):
Book 1-Strax and the Widow
Book 2-Revenge and Machinery
Book 3-From Lafayette to London

More Society Steampunk Stories (revised):
A Long Reign, The Society Travelers Series, v.1
The Kicho, The Dolls of Society, v.1
A Dream of Emerald Skies, A Young Society Series, v.1

The Brown Lady, Short Story Edition

The Vampire's Little Black Book Series (revised): v. 1-15

The Vermilion Countess Series

A Book of Sleepy Dogs

ABOUT THE AUTHOR

Victoria L. Szulc is a multi-media artist and author. Victoria's work has been recognized in St. Louis Magazine (2019 A-List Reader's Choice Author 2nd Place winner), Amazon UK Storytellers 2017 semi-finalist, the Museum of the Dog, and her illustrations of Cecilia for "Cecilia's Tale" won a runners up award for The Distinctive Cat Stephen Memorial Award 2019.

Inspired by the works of Beatrix Potter, the Bronte sisters, Jane Austen, C.S. Lewis, and Ian Fleming, she "lives" her art through various hobbies including: drawing, writing, volunteering for animal charities, yoga, voice over work, and weather spotting. She specializes in pet portraiture through her company The Haute Hen.

For character development she's currently learning/researching chess, fencing and whip cracking. Victoria blogs about these adventures at: mysteampunkproject.wordpress.com

and

https://haute-hen-countess.square.site/

"Adventures abound and romance is to be had."

-*Victoria*

Made in the USA
Monee, IL
27 August 2022